Penn Shirley

The Happy Six

Penn Shirley

The Happy Six

ISBN/EAN: 9783337407629

Printed in Europe, USA, Canada, Australia, Japan

Cover: Foto ©Andreas Hilbeck / pixelio.de

More available books at **www.hansebooks.com**

THE SILVER GATE SERIES

THE HAPPY SIX

BY

PENN SHIRLEY

AUTHOR OF "LITTLE MISS WEEZY" "LITTLE MISS WEEZY'S BROTHER" "LITTLE MISS WEEZY'S SISTER" "YOUNG MASTER KIRKE" "THE MERRY FIVE" ETC.

ILLUSTRATED

BOSTON:

LOTHROP, LEE & SHEPARD CO.

The Happy Six

Norwood Press
J. S. Cushing & Co. — Berwick & Smith
Norwood Mass. U.S.A.

CONTENTS

LIST OF ILLUSTRATIONS.

THE HAPPY SIX

CHAPTER I

FIVE AND ONE

"The Happy Six" grew out of "The Merry Five," and this was the way of it:—

The Merry Five, as you may remember, were Molly, Kirke, and Weezy Rowe, and their twin neighbors, Paul and Pauline Bradstreet; and they lived in Silver Gate City, in sunny California.

Well,—to go on with the story,—one May morning before school-time, as Kirke was amusing his little brother upon the veranda, Molly came rushing out in great excitement, crying,—

"O Kirke, you can't guess what's going to happen to The Merry Five!"

Kirke, engaged in attaching a string to the neck of a speckled horned toad, answered coolly without looking up,—

"No; and I never said I could. Fortune-telling is not my trade."

"What *is* your trade, you funny boy?" asked little Miss Weezy, suddenly appearing from the garden.

"Just at present I am in the harness business," he returned, as he tied together the ends of the cord.

Yellow-haired Donald, on his hands and knees at his brother's feet, watched the proceeding with deep interest, for this toad was to be his little pony.

"In the teasing business you mean, Kirke Rowe," retorted Molly, tossing back her long auburn braid with some impatience. "You want me to think you don't care what happens to The Merry Five."

"Whisper it to *me*, Molly, please do!"

implored Weezy, her dainty sea-shell ear close to her sister's mouth. "I can keep a secret all to myself."

"It's not a secret," cried Molly, waltzing the child down the veranda. "It's not a secret, but Kirke needn't listen." And she chanted gayly at the top of her voice, —

> "We're going to Europe, to Europe, to Europe,
> The Merry Five are going to Europe!"

This aroused Kirke.

"Molly Rowe, what do you mean?" he cried, nearly letting the toad escape, harness and all. "Who said such a thing?"

"Well, Captain Bradstreet is going, anyway. There's some trouble in Paris about one of his vessels: he's obliged to go in June."

"But what has that to do with us, I'd like to inquire?"

"Oh, nothing, nothing at all! Only we're going with him; that is, I almost know we are. The doctor said yesterday that papa needed a sea voyage, and mud-baths, and things. And mamma said just now, 'Yes, Edward, you ought to go to Europe.' And when mamma says that"—

"I declare, Molly Rowe, it does look like it! June, did you say?"

"Is it far to Europe?" asked Weezy anxiously; "farther than Mexico?"

"Farther than Mexico? Why, you little goosie, Mexico is within sight of us, and Europe is 'way off to the other side of the world."

"Truly? Then I'm not going to any old Europe!"

And Weezy's lip began to quiver.

"Not with papa and mamma, darling?" said Molly. "They'll go with us and so will Captain Bradstreet, and they'll all take care of The Merry Five."

"Here's three cheers for Europe!" shouted Kirke, swinging his cap. "And hurrah! Three cheers for The Merry Five!"

"Hurrah! *Free chairs for Mary Five!*" echoed little Donald, flapping his arms like a windmill in a gale. "Hurrah! Free chairs for Mary Five!"

It was so droll to hear him that his listeners all laughed: and who can wonder?

"Bravo, Don!" roared Kirke, tossing the little cheerer over his shoulder. "If your *Mary Five* wants *free chairs* she ought to have 'em!"

"So I say," said Molly, drying her eyes. "And a little boy that can shout for her like that deserves a reserved seat!"

"Let's give him one—a reserved seat in our club," returned Kirke good-naturedly. "He ought to come into The Merry Five."

"Only with him, you see, we shouldn't be The Merry Five any longer," demurred Molly; "there'd be one to carry."

"Then we might call ourselves The Merry *Six:* how is that?" amended Kirke, setting

Donald down again. "What do you say to The Merry Six?"

"The Merry Half Dozen would be nicer, *I* think," put in Weezy; "a great deal nicer."

"Nonsense, Weezy," retorted Kirke, "that sounds like a nestful of eggs! Let's have it The Merry Six."

"Why not The *Happy* Six?" asked Molly, with a roguish smile. "Let's be happy now, just for a change."

"Agreed, Molly, I'm willing, if Paul and Pauline are."

"So am I, too," assented Miss Weezy, though secretly preferring a half dozen to six.

Paul was just now away on a visit, but when they proposed the question to Pauline that afternoon, she received "little Number Six" into the club with open arms, and declared that his extreme youth was no objection whatever. She had heard that as people grow older, they always approve of having young members come into their clubs. She was sure Paul would welcome Master Donald cordially, and would agree with them all that the new name proposed by Molly was exactly the thing.

Thus it happened that Donald and his "Mary Five" became straightway "The Happy Six;" and this is a true account of the transaction; though, to be sure, it had not been settled yet that the club was going to Europe.

"But what difference does that make?" asked Pauline. "Can't we be The Happy Six, all the same, wherever we are? I move that we try to be happy right here in California till the middle of June, anyway, and then"—

"I second the move," responded Molly.

"'Tis a vote," cried Kirke and little Number Six in chorus.

And now, in the chapters that follow, you will hear more of this new brother-and-sister-hood, and will learn of its whereabouts and all its proceedings.

CHAPTER II

SHOT AND SING WUNG

WHETHER the Rowes should decide to go to Europe or not, the Bradstreets were going; and Captain Bradstreet thought it high time to inform Paul of the plan. The boy had not been well for some days, and for change of air had been sent to the ranch of Mr. Keith, a relative, who had a warm regard for himself and his sister Pauline.

"Kirke," said the captain, driving up that afternoon after school, "I'm going out to Mr. Keith's to see Paul. Would you like to go with me?"

"Thank you, thank you, Captain Bradstreet, I'll be ready in a second," cried Kirke, rushing for his hat.

The spirited horse had been reined up to the hedge, where he pawed and champed the bit, till his passenger appeared and vaulted headlong into the phaëton.

In his haste, Kirke had forgotten to tie Shot, the fox-terrier, into his kennel.

"Weezy, Weezy," he called over his shoulder, as the carriage started. "Look out for Shot, please, Weezy; don't let him follow us."

"I won't let him," said Weezy; "I'll keep him." And she drew him into the house and closed the door.

Having done this, she went back upon the veranda to finish her sewing. She was making a golf cape for her pet doll to wear at sea; and the work proved so absorbing that she failed to notice what Donald was doing. Before she knew it, the child had opened the front door, and run into the hall; and at the same time Shot had run out, and gone tearing after the phaeton.

Kirke looked rather crestfallen when the little animal came barking about the wheels.

"There's that dog, after all. I didn't mean he should come."

"Send him home, then," suggested the captain. "Why don't you send him home, Kirke?"

"Because he wouldn't go," answered the lad, in laughing confusion. "He wouldn't go, and I should only hurt his feelings for nothing."

The ruddy-faced captain suppressed a smile, and listened patiently, while Kirke proceeded to sing the praises of the graceful white terrier, who would not obey his master.

"He loves me tremendously; he can't bear to stay away from me: there's the trouble."

And in truth a more affectionate dog than little Shot never lived. He was a general favorite, which certainly could not have been said of Zip, Donald's Mexican cur that had died the preceding autumn.

As the phaeton whirled along, Shot darted first to one side of the road and then to the other, to chase squirrels and gophers into their holes, but without once losing sight of his beloved owner.

"I suppose, Kirke, you're very fond of the little rascal," observed the captain, as they drew near the end of their drive.

"You'd better believe I am, Captain Bradstreet. I wouldn't part with him for a farm."

"The lad's in sober earnest," thought the gentleman, peering from beneath his white eyebrows at Kirke's animated face. "I never knew a boy more devoted to his friends."

They were now spinning along the winding avenue leading to Mr. Keith's house. At their right was a green lawn, bordered with orange-trees; on their left, a thrifty olive-orchard, in which a Chinaman was plowing.

"They're always plowing somewhere," commented the captain. "I understand the soil has to be turned over pretty often to keep it light and moist."

"And it has to be irrigated, too, doesn't it?" asked Kirke, watching Shot, skipping nimbly across the field toward the mule-team.

"Irrigated? Oh, yes. But there's not water enough at present to do the thing thoroughly, and that is why Mr. Keith is having a new well dug over yonder."

"I see it," said Kirke, glancing in the direction indicated by the captain; "and he has got the curb up already."

"So he has. Ah, here comes Paul. I"—

The sentence was cut short by a prolonged howl from Shot. The confiding little creature had ventured too near the Chinaman's heels, and Sing Wung, suspecting him of evil intentions, had driven him away by a vigorous kick.

"The old wretch!" cried Kirke, springing over the carriage-wheel. "He's been abusing my poor little Shot!"

And as the yelping dog ran up to him for protection, Kirke soothed him as he would have soothed a baby.

Before Captain Bradstreet could hitch his horse to the post under the pepper-tree, Paul was beside him, his face aglow with pleasure as well as with sunburn. The sunburn caused him to look more than ever like his father. Each had large, frank, blue eyes and a ruddy complexion; but while the captain's hair was snow-white, his son's was flaxen, or, as Pauline would have it, "a light *écru*."

"How are you, Paul? How are you, my dear boy? Better, I hope?"

"Oh yes, papa, ever so much better, thank you. But why haven't you come before? I've looked for you and looked for you!"

Paul spoke with feeling. He and Pauline, though now fifteen years of age, were not ashamed to show their love for their father. The affection existing between Captain Bradstreet and his motherless twins was something beautiful to behold.

Kirke was surprised to see how coolly Paul received the news of the proposed trip to Europe. Though greatly pleased, he was by no means as excited as Kirke had been that morning when the plan was first mentioned. Paul was a quieter sort of boy than Kirke, and two years older. Moreover, he had already been to sea several times, and the novelty was pretty well worn off. Still, he wished to go again very much, especially if the Rowes would go, too, for "that would make it a good deal jollier."

After chatting awhile, Captain Bradstreet went into the lemon-house to speak with his cousin, Mr. Keith, leaving the boys to entertain each other. Paul, acting as host, at once invited Kirke to visit the well that had been begun; and they sauntered by the lemon-grove to a deep hole sunk in the ground. Above the hole stood a windlass with a bucket attached to it.

"Is anybody down there now?" asked Kirke, dropping upon his knees and peering into the dark cavern.

"No, Yeck Wo is sick to-day; so Sing Wung left off working here, and is cultivating in the orchard."

"So it takes two to run this thing?"

"Yes. Sing Wung stays below to shovel earth into the bucket, and Yeck Wo stays up here to turn the windlass and draw the bucket up into daylight."

"I see," said Kirke, "and the Wo fellow tips the earth out of the bucket on to this heap here, then sends the bucket back empty. It must be fun to watch him."

"It'll be more fun, though, when they strike hard pan, for then they'll begin to blast."

It was not Paul who said this, but Mr. Keith. He and Captain Bradstreet had now joined the boys and were standing with them near the well. "When they begin to blast, Kirke, you must come down here and make us a little visit," added Mr. Keith.

Kirke accepted the invitation eagerly, for, like most boys of thirteen, he revelled in the explosion of gunpowder.

"Let's see, can't you come Saturday, bright and early? I've promised to let Sing Wung go home Friday, and Paul will drive out for him Saturday morning, and could bring you back with him as well as not."

"O Mr. Keith, I *hope* I can come," said Kirke joyously, as he and the captain took their departure.

But in repassing the olive-orchard the youth's happy face clouded. In the distance he caught a glimpse of Sing Wung in the very act of flinging a stone at little Shot, who, forgetful of the recent repulse, had frisked again into his neighborhood.

"If that old Chinaman wasn't so far off I'd give him 'Hail Columbia!'" muttered he. "Mean creature! Wouldn't I like to dump him into that new well?"

"No; you certainly wouldn't," said the captain with an indulgent smile. "On the contrary, I'll wager that if he should fall in, you'd be the first to help pull him out."

Kirke was indignantly protesting that he "should do no such thing," when suddenly the horse, Pizarro, stumbled upon a rolling stone and turned a half-somersault down the hill.

In an instant Captain Bradstreet and Kirke had leaped to the ground.

"Sit upon his head, Kirke," ordered the captain. "So long as his head is kept down he can't flounder about."

Kirke did as he was told, and while he was perched upon Pizarro's broad cheek, Captain Bradstreet unbuckled the harness and detached it from the phaeton.

"The thill is broken, isn't it?" asked Kirke.

"Yes, broken almost in two."

Captain Bradstreet firmly grasped the horse's bridle. "Now jump, Kirke, and be quick about it."

Kirke promptly obeyed, and Pizarro straightway struggled to his feet, looking very much ashamed.

"He doesn't seem to be injured anywhere," said the captain, after carefully feeling the horse's limbs. "I wish the same could be said of the phaeton. Have you a string about you, Kirke, to splice that shaft with?"

For a wonder Kirke's pocket to-day did not boast of even so much as a fishing-line.

"I might run to the next ranch and beg a bit of rope," he suggested.

"Wait a moment, my boy, here comes a greaser. Let's see what he can do for us."

A "greaser" is the common name for a Mexican Indian.

"What an ugly, stupid-looking fellow," thought Kirke; "I don't believe he knows a string from a rattlesnake."

But, unpromising as he appeared, the Indian understood a little English, and, on being offered a silver quarter, uncoiled from his neck a long, narrow strip of deerskin, and with it tied together the splintered ends of the thill.

"The greasers use those strips of deerhide when they tote bundles on their backs," explained the captain, when they were again on their way. "He has spliced the shaft pretty firmly, Kirke, but it may draw apart. You'd better keep close watch of it."

The damaged thill was the one on Kirke's side of the phaeton, and for the rest of the drive he felt such a responsibility about it that he forgot everything else; he even forgot his beloved little terrier.

They were entering the city before he noticed that Shot was nowhere in sight. Then he remembered that he had not seen him since leaving Mr. Keith's ranch.

"Now I think of it, I haven't seen him either," said Captain Bradstreet. "Maybe the little scamp took a notion to stay with Paul."

"Oh, no, Captain Bradstreet, that wouldn't be a bit like Shot!" exclaimed Kirke vehemently. "Don't you know how he's always tagging after me?"

"Yes, like a dory after a pilot-boat," said the captain, smiling.

"Where can he be, I wonder? Do you suppose — you *don't* suppose — that hateful Chinaman can have lamed him or anything?"

Kirke looked so extremely troubled that

the tender-hearted captain hastened to reply, "No, indeed! I don't suppose anything of the kind. More likely Shot has picked a quarrel with a gopher and is bound to have the last word. If he's not at home by sunrise we'll ride back to the ranch to look him up."

He fully expected to hear the dog's merry bark at any moment, and was quite disturbed the next morning when Kirke ran over to tell him that the little terrier was still missing.

"Don't worry, we'll soon find him," he said; and immediately telephoned for the horse and surrey.

But when he and Kirke reached the ranch Shot was not there, nor had he been there since the previous afternoon. "The very last I saw of him, Sing Wung was shying a stone at him," said Paul. "He hates dogs, that Chinaman does. I believe he's afraid of them."

"He couldn't have been afraid of my dear little innocent terrier," exclaimed Kirke savagely; "he stoned him just for meanness."

On being interviewed, Sing Wung protested that the dog had followed the carriage, and that was all he knew about him. But he spoke in such a hesitating way that Kirke was sure he kept back the truth. The lad was passing through a fiery ordeal and his heart was hot within him. "If ever I saw lies I saw 'em to-day in those slanting eyes behind us," he said in Paul's ear as they turned away from the suspected Celestial. "I feel just as if he had killed poor little Shot and pitched him into the cañon."

"Oh, he wouldn't do that, Kirke; 'twould take too much courage—Sing Wung is a chicken-hearted creature."

"Not too chicken-hearted to stone my dog, though."

Paul could not gainsay this, but as he bade Kirke good-by, he remarked cheerily, —

"I half believe you'll find Shot at home waiting for you. I shall know Saturday morning. Remember I'm coming for you Saturday morning at six o'clock, sharp."

CHAPTER III

WHO WAS THE THIEF?

PAUL called for Kirke on the following Saturday, long before breakfast-time. He had driven in from the ranch in Mr. Keith's two-seated wagon, drawn by a pair of little brown mules, and was evidently in a prodigious hurry.

"Hello, Selkirk!" he shouted to the side of the house. "Stir around lively. Mr. Keith wants Sing Wung to get to work on the well early."

"I'll be there in two seconds," returned Kirke, thrusting a tumbled head through an open window. "All dressed but my hair."

"Good! Can't you eat your breakfast on the road?"

"To be sure. I can eat anywhere, everywhere."

The tumbled head disappeared; and Paul began to munch a buttered roll just brought him by his sister Pauline. Their home was just across the street, and she had watched for Paul, and rushed out to meet him, and now stood leaning against the front wheel of the wagon, chatting with him. She was a warm-hearted, impulsive girl, rather too heedless and outspoken at times. She had no mother to guide her, and lacked the gentle manners of her friend, Molly Rowe.

"You ought to put on your hat, Polly. You're getting as brown as a Mexican," remarked Paul, with brotherly frankness, as he attacked a second roll.

"Black, you should say," corrected she coolly. "I've noticed it myself. You're an albino. I'm a negress. I've no manner of doubt people call us 'the black and white twins.'"

"What about Shot, Paul? Has he been heard from?" called Molly from behind the window-shade of her chamber.

"Oh, I hoped he had turned up by this time. No, we haven't seen a sign of him, Molly; but we've found this."

Here Paul held up a dog's collar.

"Shot's collar!" cried Molly.

"You don't mean to say you've found that and haven't found the dog?" exclaimed Kirke, rushing down the steps of the veranda, flourishing in one hand a gripsack, in the other a small bunch of bananas. "Where did you find it, Paul? And when?"

"Last night, Kirke, in the hedge of the olive-orchard."

"In the hedge?"

"Yes, tucked under it, 'way out of sight."

"Then somebody hid it there—Sing Wung! I'll bet 'twas Sing Wung!" muttered Kirke, as he mounted the wagon. "He killed Shot. Got mad with him and killed him, and then saved his collar. He thought he could get money for it."

"Has somebody killed Shot?" piped half-dressed Weezy, screening herself from view behind her sister. "Oh, dear, dear! Poor little Shot!"

"Deah, deah, poo' 'ittle S'ot!" echoed Don, running to the casement in his ruffled white night-dress, and standing there quite unabashed.

"Such a sweet, lovely little dog as he was!" went on Weezy, in a tearful voice. "Just as white and good as he could be. S'pose he's got up to heaven yet, Kirke?"

"The idea, Weezy!" Kirke's tone was at once grieved and scornful. "Who ever heard of a fox-terrier's going to heaven?"

"Don't good little fox-terriers go to heaven? Nobody ever told me that before," sighed Weezy, as Paul turned the mules toward Chinatown. "O Kirke, don't you wish Shot had been a good little skye-terrier 'stead of a fox? He would have gone to heaven *then*, you know!"

"It's no sign Shot is dead, Weezy, dear, because he just happened to lose his collar," cried Pauline, stepping back from the wheel with a smothered laugh. "He'll come trotting home, wagging his tail, one of these days, you'll see!"

It was like Pauline to prophesy pleasant things. She was always hopeful, always cheerful. They called her the merriest member of The Happy Six.

"Yes, Polly, and you'll see, too," was Kirke's gloomy rejoinder. "Good-by, everybody."

"Good-by, Sobersides," retorted Pauline, brushing her sleeves, which had rested upon the dusty tire. "Good-by, Twinny, love, I'll be happy to meet you later in Europe, both of you."

Kirke hardly smiled at this nonsensical farewell. He cared very little just now about Europe, or any other foreign country. He could only think of Shot's collar found in the hedge. Somebody had hidden it there; and in his heart Kirke convicted Sing Wung.

"That collar was expensive, you know, Paul," he broke forth, before they had reached the first corner. "He was going to sell it at one of the second-hand stores."

"How could he have sold it? That would have given him away, Kirke. Shot's name is on it."

"Poh! couldn't the villain have ripped off that plate?"

"Not very easily. Besides, Kirke, if Sing Wung really meant to sell the collar, why didn't he carry it home with him yesterday?"

"Perhaps he couldn't screw his courage up. He might have been afraid of getting caught taking it."

Though by nature unsuspicious, Kirke was a boy of strong prejudices. Since making up his mind that the Chinaman was guilty of a crime, he could no longer tolerate him.

"But how are we going to prove that Sing Wung put the collar in the hedge?" asked Paul earnestly. "Mr. Keith says it isn't fair to condemn *anybody* on circumstantial evidence."

"Fudge! What more evidence does he want? Didn't we both see Sing Wung stoning my Shot? And has anybody set eyes on my Shot from that day to this?"

"No," said Paul, "it does look dark against Sing Wung, I confess, and I'm just as mad with him as you are."

"I shouldn't think Mr. Keith would keep such a sneak. He ought to discharge him, and I've a great mind to tell him so," returned Kirke, as if his opinion and advice would carry great weight with that gentleman.

"Oh, he can't discharge him now, Kirke! How can he, right in the height of the barley harvest?"

"He can hire somebody else."

"No, he can't for love or money. The Mexicans and Chinamen are all engaged for the season by this time. Besides, there's the well not half done."

Kirke bit his lip. He knew that this well was needed at once. He had seen for himself how Mr. Keith's young orange-trees were turning yellow for want of proper irrigation. As they approached the Chinese quarter of the city, he broke the silence by remarking grimly, —

"I sha'n't speak to Sing Wung. I want him to know I suspect him."

"Do you suppose he'll take the *cue?*" asked Paul, attempting his sister's trick of punning.

Sing Wung was waiting for them at the door of his whitewashed cabin. He was dressed as usual in loose blue trousers and a frock of lighter blue denim, his long cue wound about his head in a coil and tied with narrow, indigo-colored ribbon.

"He has the blues awfully, hasn't he?" whispered Kirke, not to be outdone by Paul in the play upon words.

"One of his relatives must have died," was Paul's low answer as he drew in the reins. "I've heard that the Chinese wear blue ribbon on their hair for mourning."

"If he's mourning for my dog, it looks well in him," mused Shot's bereaved master; and to emphasize his indignation Kirke turned away his head while Sing Wung climbed to the back seat of the wagon.

Paul cracked the whip, and the grotesque little mules trotted on, flapping their broad ears at every step, as if they considered them wings and were preparing to fly.

"The grass is getting brown," remarked

Paul, when they had left the city behind them, "as brown as hay. And phew! isn't the road dusty!"

"Sneezing dusty," answered Kirke; "I don't believe the people that live in that shanty over yonder have to spend any money for snuff."

As he spoke he pointed to a wretched hut a little removed from the highway, and entirely surrounded by dirt.

"Mateo lives there," said Paul carelessly.

"Who's Mateo?"

"Mateo? Oh, he's a lazy, no-account Indian, who helps sometimes on the ranch."

"I wonder if he isn't the fellow that mended our thill for us the other day?" mused Kirke. "We broke down somewhere near here. How does he look? Is he fat?"

"Fat as butter. He ought to be, you know, considering they call him a *greaser*."

Kirke giggled, and Paul looked highly gratified at the success of his witticism. He thought he might get up quite a reputation as a humorist, if Pauline didn't always say the funny things before he had a chance. He was glad to feel that he was entertaining Kirke: he couldn't bear to see the boy so downhearted.

The mules were frisky that morning, and reached the end of the journey in excellent season.

"Heap soon!" grinned Sing Wung, as he alighted upon the ground, apparently not at all disturbed because Kirke had taken no notice of him whatever.

"Oh, you can laugh, can you?" thought Kirke, hopping down over the opposite wheel. "You ought to be howling, you dog-murderer!"

"You're early, Sing Wung," said Mr. Keith, who had come out to shake hands with the boys. "You've got ahead of Yeck Wo."

"Hasn't Yeck Wo come yet?" asked Paul

quickly. "You don't suppose the man is sick again, do you, Mr. Keith?"

"I'm beginning to fear it, Paul."

"If he is, what's to be done, Mr. Keith?"

Paul still stood by the wagon, reins in hand. He was very much interested in the progress of the well, and wanted the digging to go on, since Kirke had come on purpose to watch it.

"Sha'n't I go for Mateo, Mr. Keith?"

"No, Paul, thank you, not quite yet. I don't want Mateo as long as there's any hope of Yeck Wo. But if Yeck Wo doesn't come, I may ask you later to go for Mateo. We'll tie the mules here under the pepper-tree to have them handy."

"No workee?" asked Sing Wung, not quite understanding what was said.

"Yes, yes, Sing Wung, you can go right to work here," said Mr. Keith, leading the way to the new well. "Come boys, please, and help me lower him down in the bucket. He must go to digging."

The boys sprang forward with alacrity, feeling that now the fun had fairly begun.

CHAPTER IV

KIRKE'S BRAVE DEED

SWINGING his limber arms, the little blue clad Chinaman scuffed behind Mr. Keith and the boys to the mouth of the unfinished well. Over this stood the temporary windlass, its huge bucket swaying to and fro above the dizzy hollow.

Kirke noticed that this hollow was deeper than when he had seen it last, and the mound of loose earth near it was considerably higher.

Mr. Keith and the two boys held the crank of the windlass with an iron grip while Sing Wung stepped inside the bucket; then turning the handle slowly backward, they lowered him deeper and deeper till he had reached the bottom of the dim-yawning cave.

"I told Captain Bradstreet I'd like to dump Sing Wung into this well, and I've done it," said Kirke aside to Paul.

"The slant-eyed old villain doesn't weigh much more than your little Shot," responded Paul, bending over the dusky abyss.

By this time the Chinaman had scrambled out of his novel elevator and was throwing into it great spadefuls of dirt.

Mr. Keith looked at his watch. "I begin to think Yeck Wo isn't coming. If he lived anywhere near, I'd send to inquire."

At that moment Sing Wung piped shrilly from beneath their feet.

"Heap muchee! Pullee! Pullee!"

Kirke sprang to the windlass, crying, "Lend a hand, Paul. You and I together can hoist the bucket."

"You're very kind, boys," said Mr. Keith gratefully, as he assisted them in emptying the dirt. "We'll take turns at this business for a little while, if you're willing. Yeck Wo may soon be here. He's worth two Mateos."

For a half hour the work went on briskly, Sing Wung in the depths below filling the bucket, and Mr. Keith and his young aids above ground hauling it to the surface and there dumping its contents.

Then suddenly was heard a sharp, metallic sound, — the scraping of the Chinaman's spade against a rock.

"He's struck hard pan," shouted the excited lads in a breath. "Hurrah! Hurrah! Sing Wung has struck hard pan."

"You're right, boys, I believe you're right," cried Mr. Keith, hardly less excited than they. "Next thing we may come to water."

"Are you going to blast now, Mr. Keith? Shall I bring you the drills and hammer?" asked Paul eagerly.

"Yes, Paul, if you please, and a stick of giant powder and the caps and that coil of fuse."

After these articles had been dropped into the well, Sing Wung began the process of drilling, using the shortest drill first, and longer and longer ones as he pierced farther and farther into the hard pan. He worked quickly, turning the pointed steel instrument a little with his left hand each time he struck its blunt top with the hammer.

Having assured himself of the Chinaman's skill, Mr. Keith soon shouted to him, "Call me as soon as the hole is three feet deep," and followed by the boys walked away for a drink of cool water from the Mexican *olla* on the veranda.

"It will take the man two hours at the least," he remarked, as he reached for the gourd, "and perhaps half a day. There is nothing yet for Mateo to do."

In about two hours and a half they were summoned by the sharp voice of Sing Wung. He had finished the drilling and awaited further instructions.

"The next thing to do, Sing Wung, is to fit one of those percussion caps to the end of the fuse," cried Mr. Keith, when he had reached the surface of the well.

"Yah!" growled Sing Wung, like an imprisoned bear beneath.

"Well, now tie the fuse into the paper wrapped around the stick of powder. Do you hear?"

"Yah!" louder than before.

"A half stick of the giant powder will be enough. Then drop the powder, cap, and fuse into the hole, and press down with a lot of dry earth. Do you understand?"

"No tellee! Makee holee all samee," muttered the Chinaman sulkily. Had he not blasted hard pan before?

"Then cut off the fuse about four feet from the hole, Sing Wung."

They heard the Chinaman yawn noisily, as if to say, "Melican man muchee talkee"; but Mr. Keith continued, undaunted,—

"And when everything is ready, Sing Wung, set fire to the end of the fuse and jump into the bucket. We'll pull you up in a hurry."

"Allee yight!"

Sing Wung understood perfectly. He was already cutting in two a stick of giant powder. In a short time he had buried this, as directed, lighted the fuse, and been drawn up out of the well.

The four ran to a safe distance, and two minutes later came a loud explosion. Sing Wung, after the dust and smoke had cleared away, was again let down to his work. He carried in his arms a can of black gunpowder.

"If Mateo were here to lower me, I'd go down myself to see the size of the chamber made in the rock," said Mr. Keith. "I don't know about trusting Sing Wung's judgment in regard to the amount of powder to use."

"Kirke and I can let you down, Mr. Keith," volunteered Paul promptly.

"Yes, indeed," rejoined Kirke. "I can lift as much as Paul can."

"I know you're strong for your age, Kirke, but I weigh over two hundred pounds. I'm afraid you boys might let me down in too great a hurry."

"No, no, Mr. Keith, we'll promise not to drop you."

Nevertheless, after the gentleman, against his better judgment, had been prevailed upon to enter the bucket, he looked so overgrown in it — like an oak-tree in a tub — that the boys could hardly manage the windlass for laughing.

Landed at last in safety upon the bed-rock,

Mr. Keith found that the hole drilled by the Chinaman had been enlarged by the giant powder to the size of a great kettle. Into this hole he poured about four quarts of black gunpowder and inserted the end of a fresh fuse. Finally he filled the rest of the cavity with fine dry earth and "tamped" this down very firmly.

"I've put in a heavy charge, Sing Wung," he said, as he turned from the man and stepped back into the bucket. "After you've lighted the fuse, you must run for your life. You mustn't go to sleep."

"All yightee, no sleepee!" responded the Chinaman, who, notwithstanding his oblique eyes, could sometimes see a joke.

"The Chinese ought to understand gunpowder, considering that they invented it," remarked Mr. Keith, as he emerged into the upper air. "I hope I sha'n't have to go underground again to teach Sing Wung."

The boys secretly echoed this hope, having found their host's weight a severe strain to their muscles.

That this weight had been also a severe strain upon the rope — not a new one — had not occurred to them or to Mr. Keith, or, indeed, to Sing Wung himself.

"It is evident that Yeck Wo is not coming," said Mr. Keith again, consulting his watch. "After this next explosion there will be a great deal of hard pan to be hoisted out, and we must have Mateo to help us. If you'll bring him, Paul, I'll be much obliged."

Paul went, and was away some time. Before his return Sing Wung had finished drilling the hole in the rock and begun to put in the charge. Mr. Keith and Kirke had let the bucket down to the bottom of the well and stood ready to turn the windlass at a second's notice.

Suddenly a faint light glimmered in the

darkness below, and the Chinaman leaped into the bucket yelling, —

"Pullee! Pullee!"

He had just ignited the fuse, and as the flame crept slowly along its tube the gunpowder interwoven in its fibres gave out a quick succession of snapping sounds.

"Hold on, Sing Wung, we'll pull you out in no time!" Mr. Keith shouted back; and he and Kirke turned the crank with a will.

But, alas! at the second revolution of the windlass the rope broke, dropping the bucket and its living freight back into the well!

Half-crazed by the accident, Sing Wung struggled to his knees with a piercing cry, and glared at the fire which drew every moment nearer, hissing and crackling.

"Step on it! Put it out, man! Quick, quick! are you crazy?" shrieked Mr. Keith, leaning down into the well at the risk of losing his balance.

The unfortunate wretch was so paralyzed with fright that he seemed powerless to obey. He could only cower upon the rocks below, muttering and mumbling.

"Good heavens, Kirke, he'll be blown to inch-pieces! Where are his wits?" ejaculated Mr. Keith, rushing to the porch for the olla in the frantic hope of quenching the spark with water. To his dismay the jar was empty.

Kirke, left to his own devices, roared to Sing Wung, "Try to catch hold of the rope! Hang on to it! I'll draw you up!"

But the frenzied creature never raised his eyes from that fascinating spark creeping, creeping toward the little mine of powder.

"Thunder and lightning, what ails him? I must save him if I can," thought Kirke, hastily making fast the windlass by tying down the handle.

Never pausing to consider the risk he was taking, he grasped the dangling rope and slid down upon it, hand over hand, toward the burning fuse. Should he be in season to smother it? Ah, that was the question.

When he sprang from the end of the rope to a foothold upon the rock beside Sing Wung, the advancing flame was scarcely a finger's length from the buried powder. Even then help might be too late.

With his heart in his throat, the lad dashed forward and planted his foot upon the spark. Oh, joy! it was soon extinguished! He had saved the life of Sing Wung!

Little cared Kirke at that moment for dizzy head or blistered hands. Even his late hatred of the suspected Chinaman was quite overweighed by the intense satisfaction of having been the means of his rescue.

How Sing Wung, speedily rallying from his nervous shock, deftly spliced the severed rope; and how he and his deliverer, one after the other, were lifted from their gloomy quarters, will always remain to Kirke Rowe a blurred memory, for he had hardly returned to the sunlight before he fainted.

A dash of cold water restored him to consciousness, and he opened his eyes to find himself extended full length upon the lawn, and Mr. Keith and Paul bending anxiously over him. There were tears in both pairs of eyes, and Mr. Keith was saying in broken tones, —

"God bless the noble boy!"

And what more did Kirke see? What was that white object nestling lovingly against his breast, now lapping his cold cheek, now barking for joy? Was it, — he could hardly believe his own senses, — yes, surely, that was Shot, his dear lamented terrier!

"Why, Shot, you blessed good little dog, where have you been?" he exclaimed, starting up, all alive with happiness. "Why, Shot, where have you been?"

"He go heap far! Indian sabe!" said Sing Wung, who was squatting on his heels at Kirke's feet, and had been fanning him with a green palm leaf.

"Indian? What Indian?"

"He means Mateo," interposed Paul. "*Mateo* was the thief; he stole Shot, and now he pretends he didn't. He tries to make it out that Shot strayed to his house, and that he tied him there to keep him safe for his master."

"Keep him safe! As if my bright little dog wouldn't have known enough to go home, if he had let him alone! I don't believe one word of that old Indian's story."

"Neither do I," said Paul. "We all know better, and we told him so. See how his rope has worn the hair from Shot's neck."

"What a shame! But there, I won't fret. I have my little terrier back again, alive and well," murmured happy Kirke.

But he felt a pang of remorse, as he looked at Sing Wung, and met that Chinaman's eyes fixed upon him with a glance of the deepest devotion.

"Melican boy muchee good," said the poor fellow, brokenly. "No makee fizzee, fizzee! Sing Wung no burnee!"

"I haven't been so good to you as you think I have, Sing Wung," said honest Kirke. "But I did put out the fuse. I'm no end thankful for that!"

Still the Chinaman lingered, struggling in vain for words to tell his feelings.

"Heap glad doggee no killee," said he, at last, pointing his hook-nailed forefinger at Shot, who was at a safe distance from him. "Heap glad Melican boy no lose doggee!"

And detesting as he did the whole canine species, how could the simple Celestial have said anything to give stronger proof of his gratitude to Kirke?

CHAPTER V

OFF FOR NEW YORK

"SEEMS 's if Europe time wouldn't ever, ever come," complained Weezy again and again. For it was settled now that they were to go in June at the beginning of the summer vacation.

The golf cape for the bisque Aramenta had long been finished, and Weezy having nothing in particular to do spent hours in watching the hands of the clock.

"They go creep, creep, creepmouse, just as slow as ever they can," she said to Kirke one morning. "Can't you put some of that oil on them? I 'spect that would make them turn 'round quicker."

Kirke was in the yard cleaning his wheel,

and Weezy on the doorstep dividing her attention between him and the hall clock behind her.

"Don't look at the hands for five minutes, Weezy. See if that doesn't make them travel faster," returned Kirke, setting down his little oil-can with a knowing smile. "How would you like it yourself to have anybody staring at you every second?"

Weezy laughed. It was pleasant to have Kirke at home again. For weeks he had spent half his time out of school hours at the ranch, for of course he must see that well finished. After quite a long illness, Yeck Wo had recovered and come to the aid of Sing Wung, who could drill hard pan well enough, but would not light another fuse.

"It will never do to trust Sing Wung with gunpowder again," Mr. Keith had said in confidence to the boys; "he is too excitable, he loses his head."

From first to last the sinking of the well had caused Mr. Keith great anxiety, and it was a matter of rejoicing to him that the explosions were now safely over and the hard pan penetrated to a copious supply of water beneath.

"Shot stares at me and stares at me, and barks for nothing; but I don't mind," said Weezy, stroking the little terrier as he frisked up to her to be petted.

Kirke smiled approvingly. Shot was, indeed, a privileged character in these days and received few rebukes. He might even have been allowed to accompany his master to the Old World had not Captain Bradstreet looked upon the proposal with disfavor. Dogs were a nuisance in travelling, he said. They were a trouble and an expense, and always liable to get lost or stolen.

This settled it, and after mature reflection Kirke arranged to leave his dog and his burro with Manuel Carillo, a humble Spanish boy whom he liked very much. Manuel was fond of animals and would be kind to these, Kirke felt sure.

Kirke and Molly made numerous calls in the next few weeks, remarking to their friends, —

"We came to bid you good-by before we sail for Europe."

And everybody said, "Oh, how I wish I were going too!"

Vacation came at last, and with it the long-looked-for day of departure. The party was to go by rail to New York, and after resting in that city a week take the steamer for Havre, France.

In New York the Rowes were to visit Mrs. Tracey, Mrs. Rowe's sister, and she had promised to provide a nurse-girl to go to Europe with them and assume the care of little Donald.

It was nine o'clock in the morning when the travellers arrived at the railway station at Silver Gate City. Captain Bradstreet and Mr. Rowe checked the baggage, while Mrs. Rowe entered the car followed by The Happy Six.

"I've seen a worse-looking half-dozen before now, Mr. Rowe," whispered the captain, looking after the children with a proud smile.

"But never a merrier one, I'll warrant, Captain," returned Mr. Rowe, his eyes fixed on bright-eyed Weezy, who led the procession.

At her heels strutted little Donald in his first sailor-suit. Then came flaxen-haired Paul and his brunette sister, and behind them fair, freckled Molly and brown, wide-a-wake Kirke.

After they were all seated and the car had begun to move, Molly gave a deep sigh of satisfaction.

"We've started on our travels, Polly, do you know it?" she said with a playful pinch of her friend's arm. "Doesn't it seem too good to be true?"

That first day's ride was bliss to The Happy Six. They entertained themselves by gazing from the car window, telling stories and getting acquainted with some young girls bound for Chicago.

But when at the approach of night the colored porter came to make up the sleeping-berths, Donald cried for his own little "cribby," and objected to going to bed in "a cupboard with a curtain to it."

"'Tisn't a cupboard, it's a berth, you dear little *niggeramus*," explained Weezy; and when the others laughed at the miscalled word, she thought they were laughing at Donald.

The little maid was drowsy herself by this time, and quite willing to be helped to her own berth above that of her little brother, where she undressed behind the swaying draperies, grumbling in an undertone because the train wouldn't stop jolting while she put on her pink "slumber-wrapper." She awoke next morning grumbling at the heat of the car.

Kirke was dressed and stood waiting to take her down in his arms.

"Yes, it's warm, but what are you going to do about it, Miss? We're crossing the desert, you see, and didn't think to take along any good cool air for you to breathe."

"Kirke, Kirke, no teasing," said the mother from her seat in front of them where she sat with her bonnet on, entertaining Donald. "Weezy means to be a good girl to-day, I hope, and not to fret at what can't be helped."

"But I'm so sticky, mamma, and so dusty," murmured the little girl when she stood upon the floor.

"Yes, dear, so was I before I bathed. Look at Kirke."

After one glance, Weezy forgot her grievances and laughed outright, for dark rings of dirt had settled under her brother's eyes and a speck of soot upon the tip of his nose.

"The rest of us are ready for breakfast, Kirke, and you must hurry to make yourself presentable. The conductor says we eat at the next station."

Concealing his grimy face behind his pocket-handkerchief, Kirke rushed past the seated passengers to the men's toilet-room, while Weezy hastened to that of the women, where Molly assisted her in dressing. To comb Weezy's fine, fluffy hair was never an easy task, as she seldom stood still half a minute at a time. To-day it was peculiarly trying, because the motion of the train jolted her about even when she would have been quiet.

"Oh, oh, Molly, you are most pulling my head off!" she wailed, at a sudden lurch of the car that tangled her ringlets into the comb.

Whereupon, Molly nervously set about repairing the mischief, declaring she was sorry, and hadn't meant to hurt Weezy.

Which of the sisters suffered the more before the toilet was made, it were difficult to tell; but I rather think it was Molly; and I suspect that Molly told Pauline she did "hope the nurse girl from New York would take it upon herself to attend to that child's hair."

However, by dint of haste, Weezy was dressed at last, and on the arrival of the train at the breakfast-station the whole party went out to the dining-room and made a hurried meal.

"They are to put on a dining-car at noon, I'm happy to say, and we shall have our dinner on the train," remarked Mr. Rowe. "I dislike this rapid eating."

It was a nice dinner, well served, and The Happy Six enjoyed it immensely. They supped that night from their luncheon-basket and called it a picnic. They had adjoining tables by themselves, and the three parents were at a table farther down the aisle. They were now beyond the desert, at Laguna, where the train had been delayed for some hours by an accident to the engine.

From the window at which Paul was seated they caught a glimpse of the Indian city with its clustering adobe houses and brown church surmounted by a cross.

"Not much of a city," commented Paul, opening a box of sardines. "It looks more like a village, a tiny, half-grown one into the bargain."

"But for all that, papa says it holds thousands of Indians, just thousands!" said Kirke. "They must be packed snug, like those little fishes."

"They'd pack better if they were longer lengthwise and shorter widthwise," laughed Paul, glancing at a group of thick-set Indians parading along the track.

"Why are those red men like heavy biscuits?" asked Pauline, helping Donald to orange marmalade.

"Because they're ill-bred," responded her brother. Pauline shook her head.

"I know why they're like heavy biscuits," exclaimed Weezy confidently. "Because you can't eat 'em."

"Very bright, little Miss Weezy, but not the answer," returned Pauline amid general merriment. "Kirke, you haven't guessed. Tell me this minute why those Indians are like heavy biscuits?"

"Because"—Kirke thoughtfully squeezed lemon juice upon his sardine—"because every one of them is good for a shot."

"No, no; you're far from the mark! Molly, now it's your turn."

"Is it because they're both such a miserable lot?" asked Molly dubiously.

"Oh, you stupid guessers!" Pauline canted

her head saucily. "Why, listen now, my children. Those Indians and heavy biscuits are alike because neither have been properly raised."

"They're ill-bred, then, aren't they, just as I said," retorted Paul, twisting his neck to look at three Indian girls coming toward the car. All wore blankets, not folded, but hanging from their necks by the hems; and their flowing, black hair was straight and coarse, like a horse's mane.

"Out with your camera, Paul!" said Kirke, while Molly whispered,—

"Do look at their faces, a bright vermilion!"

"From their foreheads down to their chins. What a waste of good paint!" Kirke whispered back.

"Let's take them something to eat," said Pauline, gathering up the fragments of the luncheon.

"Yes, yes, so we will," cried Molly.

And the gay little party hurried forth to feed the young squaws, and buy some of the curious specimens of rocks they had brought to sell.

Paul seized the opportunity to take a "snap-shot" at the dusky damsels. Kirke purchased of them several bits of colored stone for his cabinet, and remarked later to Paul that if those squaws couldn't speak English, they could tell a nickel from a dime with their eyes shut.

This meeting with the Indians was a pleasant experience to The Happy Six,—a much pleasanter one than that which Kirke was doomed to pass through on the morning they entered New York.

Kirke's experience occurred in this wise: The night before they reached New York he and Paul occupied a section at the front of the sleeping-car next the door, Paul having the lower and Kirke the upper berth.

After undressing, Kirke had rolled all his clothes together into a bundle, which he placed at the foot of his berth, where he might lay his hands on it in the morning; for he meant to be up early to see whatever was to be seen.

But when he opened his eyes at sunrise, the bundle had mysteriously disappeared.

"Paul has hidden it for a joke," was his first thought; and he leaned over the edge of his berth, and in an explosive whisper charged his comrade with the theft.

"Taken your clothes? No; what did I want of your clothes?" answered sleepy Paul, a little cross at being roused from a pleasant dream. "Why don't you ring for the porter?"

There was no mistaking the honesty of Paul's tone. Kirke began to be nervous. He pressed the electric bell by his window, and the colored porter presently appeared.

"Want anything, sah?" he asked, thrusting his woolly head between Kirke's curtains.

"Yes, porter, I want my clothes! They were in a bunch at the foot of my bed. Haven't you seen them?"

"No, sah; but I'll try to find them, sah."

Meanwhile Mr. Rowe, Captain Bradstreet, and Paul had dressed in haste, and were now ready to join in the search.

But though they hunted all through the car, their quest was in vain. The missing garments were not to be found.

"The conductor thinks the thief must have sneaked in and stolen them at the station where we stopped at midnight," said Paul, coming back to Kirke with the unwelcome news. "It seems the porter left the door unlocked a minute while he ran out to send a telegram for somebody."

"And here I am in my night-gown, Paul!

What on earth am I going to do?" groaned Kirke behind his curtains.

These were the only curtains now visible in the sleeper. The berths of all the other sections had been put up for the day.

"It's an outrageous shame, Kirke, an everlasting, heathenish shame!" vociferated Paul; but in the midst of his condolence he had to burst out laughing at the sad predicament.

Kirke relieved his own feelings by throwing a pillow at his friend. To himself the situation was far from ludicrous, it was appalling. The train was steaming on at the rate of forty miles an hour; it would soon land him in New York. Then what?

"Your father has gone to look up your trunk and get out another suit for you," continued Paul, catching his breath.

"Good! But, oh dear, how can he open the trunk without the key? The key was in my pocket!"

But the key was not needed; the baggage was not on that train.

A moment later, Mr. Rowe appeared at the section, carrying on his arm a pair of checked blue-and-white overalls.

"Well, Kirke, I've done my best for you," said he cheerily. "I've bought these of a brakeman. By rolling up the hems, I think you can manage to wear them."

"Oh, those are a bonanza, Kirke."

It was his mother's voice at the boy's elbow. "And I've brought you other things to put on. We'll leave you now to dress. Be as quick as you can."

As the train ran into the New York station, a rough-looking lad emerged from the curtains clad in a brakeman's overalls turned up at the hem, Molly's ulster, Mrs. Rowe's overshoes, and Captain Bradstreet's smoking-cap.

"O Kirke, you look like" — Mrs. Rowe

cut short Weezy's comparison by a warning glance.

"Like a California freak, Weezy. Why, I knew that; did it on purpose," retorted Kirke, assuming an air of bravado.

"Oh, no, Kirke, you look like a precious mosaic," said Pauline lightly, while the whole party managed to crowd closely about the nondescript boy.

Partially screened by his friends, the "precious mosaic" of many colors skulked along to a carriage and vaulted into it. Here the little company separated for the present, the Bradstreets proceeding to a hotel in the city, and the Rowes to the home of Mrs. Tracey, where they were to remain till the sailing of the steamer.

"Auntie'll think you're bringing her an almshouse boy, mamma," Kirke said ruefully, as they alighted before the Tracey mansion.

To greet his aunt and cousins in such a

plight, and to be laughed at the livelong day, was an embarrassing ordeal to the lad; but he bore it manfully, and if afterwards he made wry faces and stamped his foot, he did it in the privacy of his own room, and nobody was the wiser. And in the evening, with the arrival of his trunk, the prolonged and disagreeable trial came to an end.

CHAPTER VI

OFF FOR EUROPE

THE Silver Gate City party left New York the next Saturday on the French steamer *La Bretagne*, bound for Havre. They took with them Jane Leonard, a girl of eighteen, who was to have the care of Donald.

They went on board an hour before sailing, and Molly and Pauline immediately ran below deck to put in order the stateroom which they were to share with Weezy. It was a cosy, outside room near the middle of the boat, with two berths, and opposite these a cardinal velvet sofa on which Weezy was to sleep.

"It's lucky your brush-and-comb case has a loop to hang it up by, Molly," said Pauline, as they unpacked their toilet articles. "You'd better pin it to your curtain where you can reach it from your berth without raising your head."

"What for?" asked Molly, a little impatiently. She sometimes thought her friend rather too fond of dictating.

"You'll find out what for when we get into rough water and things go pitching about the vessel," responded Pauline in a significant tone. "And please, please don't put that cologne bottle in the rack. If you do 'twill rattle and dance and thump till it breaks—or you wish it would."

Molly meekly dropped the perfumery back into her hand-bag, and hung the bag upon a large hook beside the plate-glass mirror.

"You scare me to death, Polly," she said, with a shiver. "I almost wish I weren't going to sea."

"Oh, nonsense, you'll like the ocean when

you get used to its tricks," returned Pauline, with the assurance of an old sailor. "How big your eyes have grown, Miss Scared-to-death! And they are just the color of purple heliotrope."

"The washed-out kind you mean, I suppose, Polly?"

"No, I don't, I mean the washed-in kind that doesn't fade," said Pauline, giving Molly's auburn hair a vicious little pull. "You know your eyes are perfectly lovely."

"Come, girls." Mrs. Rowe appeared in their doorway from her stateroom across the passage. "Let us go on deck; the air above will be fresher."

"So it will, mamma. Besides, we want to see the land every minute we can," sighed Molly.

As they mounted the stairs of the companion-way side by side, she grasped her mother's hand and held it fast. Now that the longed-for hour of sailing had actually arrived, she felt an unexpected reluctance to leaving the solid earth behind her and trusting herself upon the heaving waters. But she said nothing more about this to Pauline. Pauline would not have understood her dread. Neither for that matter would fearless Kirke have understood it.

"I don't see your father and the others, Molly," said Mrs. Rowe rather anxiously when she and the girls stood on the crowded deck. "I hope they won't lose sight of Donald."

Pauline sprang upon a neighboring settee, where she could look down on the heads of the people.

"Jane Leonard has him over there by the rail," she cried presently. "Mr. Rowe and papa are close by them."

"Then if the child is safe, we may as well stay where we are," returned Mrs. Rowe, disposing herself upon the settee on which Molly and Pauline were now leaning.

Her words were lost in the general bustle and confusion. Soon came the cry, "All aboard!"

Visitors upon the boat rushed ashore, passengers upon the shore rushed aboard. The last to cross the gang-plank being the captain of the vessel.

Then shouts of good-by arose from the wharf, and answering shouts from the steamer; the ropes were thrown off; and with hats and handkerchiefs waving from her deck, *La Bretagne* slipped from her moorings and glided out into the harbor.

"Isn't she a beauty, Molly?" cried Pauline, tapping the back of the settee in her enthusiasm.

"Who is a beauty?"

Molly glanced over her shoulder and saw a graceful young lady seated upon a camp-stool and sorrowfully gazing at the shore.

"Oh, are you speaking of that young lady

in mourning, Polly? She's pretty, but don't you think she's too pale?"

"I was speaking of the steamboat, you dear little innocent," answered Pauline, laughing. "I hadn't noticed the other lady before. How white she is, isn't she? All the color she has is in her eyelids."

"Poor thing, she must have cried herself about blind, Polly."

At this point Captain Bradstreet came with the deck-steward to arrange the steamer-chairs of the party. Paul and Kirke followed with the shawls and travelling-rugs. Then those who wished to do so extended themselves at their ease and chatted or dozed till the dinner-bell sounded. The sea was as smooth as glass, and the only motion of the vessel was that caused by the throbbing engines.

"I'm not a bit sea-sick, boys," boasted Molly, as all went down to dinner; "I expected to be, but I'm not."

"I hope you'll not be sick during the passage," replied Paul, but his face wore a peculiar smile. It was not the first time he had heard people boast in this way before they were fairly out to sea.

On entering the dining-room, Molly saw three tables stretching from one end of it to the other, and on either side of these tables were rows of cardinal velvet chairs. Instead of being supported by four legs, each chair swung upon a pivot in a central standard screwed to the floor.

"Our seats are at the middle table," said Paul. "There are your father and mother just sitting down."

Weezy was with them and whispered to Molly as she paused beside her, —

"I tell you how to get into your chair, Molly. You squeeze in sideways and then jiggle it 'round."

"Yes, yes, Weezy, I know."

Molly wished her little sister would not make them both so conspicuous when the young lady in mourning sat next Pauline on the opposite side of the table and could hear every word.

Molly's place was between Kirke and Weezy and over against Captain Bradstreet.

"You're Number Fifteen, Molly," said Kirke, reading the black letters on his ivory napkin-ring. "You're Number Fifteen and I'm Number Fourteen."

"And I'm Number Sixteen," added Weezy, after squinting hard at her own ring.

"Yes, they treat us as if we were convicts in a state's prison," Molly turned to Kirke with a shrug. "You know they make convicts drop their own names and answer to numbers."

"I should have made a good convict, if I had worn those overalls and"—

But here Kirke was interrupted by a waiter bringing him a plate of soup.

They were a long time at dinner, which consisted of several courses and ended with harlequin ice-cream, — red, green, and white.

Donald's nurse had given her charge an early supper in the children's cabin, and when the party returned to the deck he was already in bed.

"My little brother can't stay awake after dark 'cause it makes him cross," Weezy frankly explained to the pale young lady in black with whom she had become friendly during dinner.

"Can't he? That's unfortunate," replied the young lady, smiling.

"Oh, I don't care. Not so very cross."

Weezy was eying keenly a bag of black alligator skin dangling from her companion's belt. It was rather larger than an ordinary reticule, and furnished with a steel clasp and chain. The young lady played absently with the chain while talking.

"She pets her pretty bag like a kitten. I

"'OH! I'M EVER SO SORRY,' SAID WEEZY"

Page 87

wonder what's in it?" thought Weezy, wishing it would not be rude to inquire. She suspected that it contained something very, very precious.

"Didn't anybody come with you, lady?" she questioned shyly, being exceedingly desirous to know. "Are you all *sole* alone?"

"Yes, dear; all sole alone." The speaker's voice trembled. "My father had intended to cross the ocean with me; but he was taken suddenly ill last month, and — he has died."

"Oh, I'm ever so sorry," replied Weezy, with tears in her eyes, thinking how she should feel if it were her own papa. "Haven't you any mamma?"

The young lady shook her head, not trusting herself to speak.

Weezy's hand stole quietly into that of her new friend.

"That's dreadful — not to have any papa

and mamma! Don't you want to see *my* mamma? Please come over to the other side of the boat, and I'll *induce* you to her."

"Thank you, darling; but I'd rather not go."

"My mamma's very nice," pleaded Weezy. "Her name is Mrs. Rowe. My name is Louise Rowe, only 'most all the time it's Weezy."

"I'm sure your mother must be very nice, Miss Louise. She has a lovely expression; yet, all the same, I can't intrude upon her."

"I wish you could," said Weezy, wondering what was meant by "intrude." "If you could, you wouldn't be lonesome, 'cause we have ten peoples — only Donald is abed."

"With ten in your party, Miss Louise, I'm sure you have enough *peoples* without me," responded the young lady in crape, unconsciously cheered by the child's artless sympathy. "Look, your mamma is beckoning you."

Mrs. Rowe had feared lest her sociable little daughter might annoy the stranger; but after hearing Weezy's story about her, changed her mind.

"The poor girl looks very sad and lonely," she said, watching the sweet, sensitive face, which she had observed at dinner. "I'll go back with you, Weezy, and speak to her."

And having crossed the deck, she gracefully introduced herself to the desolate young lady in mourning, who in return gave her own name as Miss Evans.

"Cannot I prevail upon you, Miss Evans, to make my little daughter and the rest of us happy, by joining us?" said Mrs. Rowe cordially. "We have a vacant seat to offer you."

There was no resisting the rare charm of the lady's manner, and the desolate stranger gladly accepted the invitation, though on being presented to the other members of the party she betrayed great shyness.

"Evidently unaccustomed to society," thought Mrs. Rowe; "yet so cultivated and refined! I can't quite understand it."

After they had become better acquainted, Miss Evans told her that her father and herself had always lived together a retired life, seeing more of books than of people. He was a scientist, and had devoted many years to preparing a learned work on biology.

"As soon as his book was finished, papa meant to take a vacation with me, Mrs. Rowe," she said tremulously. "We were to visit my uncle in Paris. But the very day after our passage on the steamer had been engaged, papa had a fatal stroke of paralysis. And so," added Miss Evans, with touching pathos, "and so I came alone."

"Alone in one sense, my dear Miss Evans; yes, sadly alone," replied Mrs. Rowe with feeling. "But please consider yourself one of our large party. Please look upon us all as your friends."

She pressed the young mourner's hand warmly as she spoke, and resolved to do all in her power to enliven her voyage.

Molly and Pauline bestowed stealthy glances upon the diffident newcomer shrouded in black in Donald's chair. In the splendor of the moonlight her pale face assumed an unearthly radiance, and Kirke remarked confidentially to Paul that she was "a regular stunner."

"Solemn as a tombstone, though," responded Paul. "And see her hang on to that bag at her belt! Anybody'd think it was a life-preserver."

"I suppose it was once, when the skin was on the alligator's back," laughed Kirke. "Hark, Paul, your father is beginning a story!"

Captain Bradstreet's stories were always

worth hearing, and the evening being warm and still, the little company was beguiled into remaining up until a late hour to listen to some of his thrilling experiences at sea.

"What delightful people these are!" thought the lonely Miss Evans. "It is such a solace to be with them. And I had not expected to speak with a soul on board."

CHAPTER VII

TEN AND ONE

THE next day the weather continued fine. The ship passed schools of porpoises sporting in the sun and splashing the water like swimming children at play.

Captain Bradstreet told Weezy that these porpoises were sometimes called fish-hogs. They not only drive shoals of herrings and salmon and mackerel before them, but they sometimes dive to the bottom of the sea and root for eels and sea-worms, as pigs on land root for acorns buried under leaves.

The second morning Paul descried a sporting whale to leeward, and an hour later an ocean steamer. When the vessels were near each other, *La Bretagne* ran up several small flags.

"Those flags ask, 'Have you seen any icebergs?'" said Captain Bradstreet.

And when the other vessel signalled by flags that the passage was clear, he seemed greatly pleased.

"I always dread to meet icebergs in a fog," he remarked.

"But there isn't a speck of fog to-day, Captain Bradstreet," put in Weezy.

"No, not yet, but we shall run into it off the Banks, little maiden."

"What banks, Captain Bradstreet?" asked Weezy, taking a peep through his spy-glass, which rested across the top of Molly's chair. "I don't see anything around here but just water."

"I mean the banks of Newfoundland, an island; but you needn't look for them, you can't see them."

"I can see something though,—something white. Look, look, Captain Bradstreet! Don't you believe it's going to begin to fog?"

"Already? Is that so?" The captain raised the glass and peered through it himself. "Yes, you're right, Bright-Eyes. The fog *is* 'going to begin' to bear down upon us."

And in a few moments the white fog had shrouded the vessel from stem to stern. Then came at frequent intervals the dreary sound of the fog-horn.

"What a hoarse old thing!" exclaimed Weezy, stopping her ears in disgust. "It brays just like Kirke's burro, only awful worse."

"As if it had a long sore throat," laughed Molly, buttoning her sister's cape at the neck.

"They're manning all the lookouts," remarked the wise Pauline.

"They're doing what, Pauline? And what are they doing it *to?*" asked Molly playfully. "Won't you please speak English?"

"Oh, you dear, stupid old land-sparrow! Don't you see those wooden cages high above the forecastle?"

"I don't know what the forecastle is; but do you mean those little platforms with fences round them?"

"Yes, those are the lookouts. There are five on this steamer, — I've counted, — and the mate has sent a sailor to each one to watch and sing out if there's danger of our running into anything."

"Ugh! I wouldn't be in their places for a hundred dollars," said Molly. "But Kirke would like it, you may depend. I never heard of such a boy! To think of the way he went down into that well to save Sing Wung!"

"Kirke is a noble little fellow," returned Captain Bradstreet heartily, to Molly's intense satisfaction. "And here he is now, coming aft, and Paul is behind him."

Pauline flirted her handkerchief at the lads as her father spoke, and they walked across the wet deck toward her, Paul slipping once on the way and nearly falling.

"A miss is as good as a mile," said his sister merrily, when he came up to her.

"Some misses are as good as two miles, if not better," said Kirke, attempting to be witty and bowing with much gallantry first to Pauline and next to Molly. "Oh, girls, I tell you we've been having fun!"

"With what, Kirke?" they both inquired. "With shuffle-board?"

"No, no, not with shuffle-board, but with —well, you might call it 'shovel-aboard,' if you want to," said Kirke, "dropping into" wit again; whereupon Paul chuckled and cried, "Pretty good, Kirke. You see we've been watching the men shovel coal into the furnace."

"Can't we go down there, too?" asked Molly, taking a step forward.

"No, indeed, not you girls! You'd spoil your dresses. Why, the furnaces are a deck below the boilers."

"And halfway down the stairs give out and you have to go the rest of the way on a ladder," added Kirke.

"It's a droll place, though, when you get there," resumed Paul. "Coal-bins all around, — they call 'em bunkers, — and stokers black as soot wheeling the coal to the furnaces in barrows."

"Stokers?" repeated Weezy. "Kirke, did I ever see a stoker? Is it a donkey?"

"Not always, little Miss Quiz," replied Kirke with a giggle; and they all laughed, as if she had said something very foolish.

"Now, I know you're making fun. I think you're as unpolite as you can be!"

Her head drooped; but before the tears could fall, Captain Bradstreet soothed her wounded feelings by whispering in her ear that little girls who had never been to sea couldn't be expected to know about stokers. He would tell her in confidence that stokers are the men who tend the fires on a steamboat.

"The poor souls weren't more than half dressed," said Paul, when peace had been restored. "But still they looked ready to melt. You never saw such a fire as they keep up in those furnaces, girls."

"Threw coal into the fire-boxes every minute or two," interposed Kirke.

Molly suddenly fell to dusting her brother's coat with her handkerchief. "You've run against something white, Kirke. And so has Paul. They don't keep their flour-barrels down there, I should hope."

"No; that's a stoker's mark. One of the stokers drew a chalk-line around our waists and said we couldn't go till we'd paid our fee."

"A stupid joke, I should call it," said Molly, for the chalk-mark was hard to remove.

"A pretty old joke," responded the captain. "They always try it on visitors. I hope you took it in good part, boys?"

"Oh, yes, papa," said Paul. "Each of us gave the man a dime."

"And made money by it, too," declared Kirke. "'Twas well worth a quarter to be let out of that hot hole."

"I'd like some of the heat up here," said Molly, her teeth chattering. "Miss Evans had to put away her writing and go below, her hands were so stiff."

"She's writing a story, Kirke, and she'll read it to me sometime. She promised she would," exclaimed Weezy, very proud of the notice she received from her new friend.

"We just met her at the foot of the companion-way with her tablet in her hand," said Kirke.

"Yes," added Paul, "and she was clutching that bag of hers, as usual. I believe she's carrying diamonds in it."

"Then you must believe her to be a very silly young woman, my son. I wonder you don't tell her that passengers are expected to give their valuables to the purser, to be locked in his safe," observed the captain jestingly. "For my part, I never should suspect that the poor girl was rolling in gold."

"I'm sure she isn't rich. She dresses very plainly," said Pauline. "By the way, what makes rich people want to 'roll,' I wonder?"

"Especially in gold," added Molly flippantly, as they entered the dining-saloon. "I shouldn't want to roll in gold, of all things. It's one of the hardest things in the world."

"And the hardest to get," broke in Paul, with a grin.

"What would you like to roll in, Molly? Soft money?" said Kirke, with a grin of his own. "That shows your politics, miss. You're a soft-money girl."

"A soft, mooney girl, Kirke Rowe? She's no such thing. I deny it!" cried Pauline, pretending to have misunderstood. "Now bring the Alphabet Bewitched, there's a good boy, and we'll have a game of letters."

With the beginning of the game, the children's lively banter ceased, and Captain Bradstreet walked off to the further end of the saloon to converse with Mr. and Mrs. Rowe.

That was the last quiet morning on board ship for three long days; for in the night a rough gale swept over the sea, tossing the vessel to and fro, and almost hurling passengers from their berths. Once Molly was awakened by a loud crash, and cried out in terror to Pauline in the upper berth.

"It's only dishes breaking in the dining-saloon," yawned Pauline, turning over. "Why don't you go to sleep?"

As her father proudly said, Pauline was a chip of the old block, a born sailor. She liked the swell of the ocean. She was never timid, never seasick. The same was true of Captain Bradstreet and of Kirke. They all went to the dining-table three times a day, sometimes five, undisturbed even though the plates might dance a jig, and the glasses in the rack above them jingle and jump and threaten to come down upon their heads.

The rest of the party, more or less ill for a time, rallied after the abatement of the storm — all of them but Weezy. When at last able to be carried on deck, she was still pale and languid, and felt rather forlorn.

The rest of the company made every effort to entertain her, but in vain. There were only two people on whom the little maid would condescend to smile. One of these was Miss Evans, who read aloud some of the delightful tales she had written; the other was a young man who never even spoke to the child; but you will hear of him in the following chapter.

CHAPTER VIII

ELEVEN IN FRANCE

Of all the passengers on the ship, — and there were perhaps six hundred, — none interested the boys of The Happy Six like the young man with one leg, who was going to London and Paris to astonish the people by his tricks on a bicycle.

He had a wife, a very pleasant young woman, and Molly and Pauline liked to talk with her. She told them she was in the habit of riding on her own wheel, ahead of her husband, and throwing balls in the air for him to fire at as he followed her; and he never failed to hit the balls.

"How wonderful!" cried Pauline.

"Yes," returned the wife proudly; "but

really not so wonderful as his spinning his wheel down a toboggan slide. That is something that has never yet been done by any man with two legs."

"Oh, I should hope not," said Molly; "it makes me shudder to think of it."

"Look, look," cried Pauline; "see what he is doing now!"

Some one was playing the fiddle, and this extraordinary young man was actually dancing in perfect time with one foot. He was laughing, too, and seemed to enjoy the performance as much as any one else.

He was always in good spirits, so his wife said; and he assured the boys that he did not mind the loss of his leg.

"There's a philosopher for you," said Mr. Rowe to Captain Bradstreet; and when the dancing was over, they both went up and shook hands cordially with the happy trick-cyclist.

And now the ship was almost at the end of her voyage. On the afternoon of the Fourth of July the deck was crowded with passengers looking pleased and expectant.

Presently across the sea to port was discerned a brown speck, and caps went up with a shout.

"What are you all making such a noise for? Tell me quick!" cried Weezy, running to the rail where Paul stood clapping his hands. By this time Weezy had quite recovered and was again her healthy, inquisitive little self.

"We've sighted Land's End, Weezy Rowe, that's what," answered Paul, with unwonted excitement.

"Oh! Oh! Are we coming to the end of the world, Paul?" Weezy's eyes sparkled like twin stars. "Are we truly, truly?"

"No, no, not to the end of the world, Miss Quizzy." Paul smothered a laugh. "We're only coming to the end of England. There's a long stretch of world beyond that."

"Oh, that's too bad!" sighed Weezy.

And as they sailed closer to the shore, she added in a tone of disapproval,—

"Land's End is a weeny bit of a thing, isn't it?"

"Not very large, Weezy. That sharp tongue is called Lizard's Point. People there are watching out and every time an ocean steamer comes in, they telegraph about it to New York."

"Why, Paul, I think that's telling tales. Can't a ship"—began Weezy; but was interrupted by this glad cry from Kirke,—

"The pilot boat! Paul, the *pi-lot* boat!"

A white-winged yacht was approaching. When it had come near enough, the steamer stopped and took the pilot on board. The passengers smiled as he mounted the rope-ladder at the vessel's side, for now they knew they should land in France the next morning. No vessel is ever allowed to land without a pilot to show her the way.

"Come, Weezy, it's time to dress for dinner," said Molly a little later, pausing in a promenade with Miss Evans. "We want to look our very best to-night, Weezy, because the captain is going to give a grand Fourth of July banquet."

"I knew that; I heard it before you did, Molly Rowe."

Weezy skipped away with her sister to their stateroom, and when the bell rang they entered the dining-saloon, arrayed in their finest apparel.

The saloon was a brilliant mass of color. American flags draped the walls; the tables were decked in red, white, and blue; and every napkin was a white tower with a small flag at its top.

"They've planted our 'Old Glory' everywhere," said Paul. "Only see!"

It was really a grand banquet and lasted a long while. With the dessert were passed little favors of colored tissue paper. Kirke's favor proved to be a blue Liberty cap which he put on with much glee. Paul and Weezy had Marie Stewart bonnets; Pauline and Molly red military hats.

After-dinner speeches followed, the French people complimenting the Americans, and the Americans complimenting the French. And then, having returned thanks to the captain for his courtesy, the guests arose from the feast.

In leaving the room Molly turned to speak with Miss Evans and observed that she had exchanged her black serge travelling dress for one of mourning silk, but still wore at her belt the large, conspicuous reticule.

"A leather bag at a grand dinner! What strange taste!" she thought. "And yet Miss Evans is certainly a lady."

In the morning they landed at the port of Havre and passed through the Custom House. There, to Weezy's great indignation, their trunks were opened and searched. When a dark, sour-looking officer handled roughly her cherished Araminta, the little girl could no longer contain herself, but in her anxiety exclaimed aloud, —

"Please, sir, lift my doll easy! Sometimes her eye falls out!"

He never answered, never even looked up, but went on holding the unfortunate Araminta upside down in his left hand, while with his right hand he fumbled about among the contents of the box.

Weezy considered his conduct extremely rude, and was very angry with him, till her mother suggested that as he was a Frenchman he might not have understood what she said.

After the luggage had been examined and

chalked with a capital letter D, our party drove to the Frascati, a large hotel, for breakfast.

After breakfast the boys walked off to the immense stone bath-house across the court. A white-capped old woman sat at a desk in the broad entrance hall, writing accounts in a ledger. The boys had French money—francs and centimes—which they had received from the purser on the ship in exchange for United States money.

Paul could speak a little French, and he bought the bath-tickets, paying an extra sum for soap and towels.

"Well, I hope that's mean enough!" said Kirke, when this was explained to him. "Do they charge extra for the water, too?"

Then they followed a waiting-maid up-stairs into separate bath-rooms; and again Kirke was astonished, for when he had entered his room, the girl turned the key and locked him in.

To the American boy, unused to foreign customs, this seemed a strange proceeding.

When he had made his toilet, rung a bell, and been released from solitary confinement, he ran out to seek Paul in the waiting-room.

"What do you think, Paul Bradstreet! That girl locked me into my room!"

"Well, she locked me into mine, too; that's a way they have in this country."

Kirke related his experience to the girls that afternoon in a very graphic way, as the quartette strolled together on the heights.

Pauline laughed, and Molly demurely remarked that she had never heard before of a country where people were shut up who hadn't been naughty!

"Be careful, Molly, or President Faure may hear you," said Paul, in pretended alarm. "I suppose he is in that square, cream-colored house this minute; it's where he lives in the summer."

"How do you know that?" asked Pauline. "Who said so?"

"The head clerk at the hotel described it to me."

"*Head clerk*, indeed! You mean *concierge*," corrected his sister. "One would think you had never been abroad before. You must use the French names."

"A queer country," said Molly. "No matter how gray-headed a man is, they call him *garçon*; and *garçon* means boy."

It had been Miss Evans's original plan to proceed directly from Havre to Paris; but on being urged by her Silver Gate friends to visit with them various points of interest along the road, she could not resist the invitation.

"I came to France mainly on account of an important errand in Paris," she said to Mrs. Rowe. "I've been wanting to tell you about it, only I can't mention the subject without crying. But now I find that the people I wish to see will be out of the city for another week or two. And so," she continued, drying her eyes, "I believe I may allow myself this pleasant holiday with you."

Accordingly she wired her uncle that he need not expect her at present, as she was to join the Silver Gate party next morning for a carriage-drive through picturesque Normandy.

CHAPTER IX

THE MYSTERIOUS BAG

THE Silver Gate tourists all assembled for breakfast in the hotel dining-room dressed for their excursion. The clothes worn by them on shipboard had been packed in a box to be forwarded to Liverpool, in readiness for the home voyage, and The Happy Six appeared now in tidy new suits. Miss Evans wore a neat black mohair and a fresh black straw hat, but had not laid aside the familiar reticule.

"The bag looks like a padlock, Paul. Do you suppose she needs all that to fasten her belt?"

"It seems like it," murmured Paul.

But the remarks were strictly confidential.

The boys would not have injured Miss Evans's feelings on any account: they were too well-bred for that. Besides, they liked her very much.

The early breakfast — or *le café* — consisted of *café au lait,* — which is coffee served with boiled milk, — rolls, and unsalted butter. This butter had been moulded into the shape of wild roses, with petals as thin as wafers, and each guest had two of these wee roses on a tiny dish beside his plate at table.

"Papa enjoys the butter, don't you see, mamma?" said Molly, in a low tone as they left the dining-room.

"Yes, I observed it," returned her mother, looking pleased. "I fancy his appetite is really improving."

Then they all mounted the black jaunting-car waiting in the court. Donald was in boisterous spirits: so delighted at his escape from the confinement of the steamer that he could hardly contain himself.

The two seats of the car ran lengthwise and faced each other. Miss Evans sat near the front, just behind the driver's box, which the voluble coachman shared with Captain Bradstreet. French *cochers* are very fond of imparting information, and this one discoursed so rapidly concerning the farms, houses, and people along the way that the captain finally turned around to Miss Evans with a comical look of despair, and said,—

"*Will* you please tell me what this man is raving about? He telescopes his words so that I can't understand him."

"He was speaking just now of these neat piles of broken stone by the roadside, Captain Bradstreet," replied Miss Evans, smiling. "He says government requires every man to furnish a given weight—I missed the number of pounds—of this crushed stone to repair the highways."

"That's why the roads look so very neat. Just the thing for bicycles. I wish they had such a law in the United States."

"I made the same remark to the *cocher*," returned Miss Evans, who seemed to talk to the man with the greatest ease.

After this, she was constantly appealed to for translating French into English. On one of these occasions, Mrs. Rowe said, with one of her affable smiles, "We are grateful to you, Miss Evans, for acting as our interpreter. Mr. Rowe and I find ourselves sadly rusty in French."

"So are Molly and I, Miss Evans," added Pauline. "You never would dream that we've just been studying it; now would you?"

"And we had good marks at school, too," said Molly. "I don't see what the trouble is."

"I do," said Pauline. "*We* are not one

bit to blame. The people don't understand their own language, that's all. Ask 'em a question, and they just shake their heads and rattle off the sounds of the vowels,—'A, ah, aw, ă, ē, e,' and so on."

Pauline was a capital mimic, and rendered this burlesque of foreign speech with a drollery that provoked loud applause and aroused Donald to a high pitch of enthusiasm.

"A, ah, ow; bow, wow wow," he screamed, waving his little hands like Pauline.

Jane Leonard quietly slipped her arm about his waist to prevent his falling from the carriage, and whispered him to be quiet, for her head ached. She considered little Number Six a very noisy child. Though too young to appreciate the quaint, beautiful pictures of the constantly changing landscape, he enjoyed their novelty, and was constantly trying to express his delight.

"And this is Normandy," said Mrs. Rowe,

drawing a long breath of satisfaction; "picturesque Normandy."

Ancient houses, on which were growing grass and flowers,—among the flowers the *fleur-de-lis*, or lily of France. By the roadside, gorgeous red poppies, hobnobbing with the blue corn-flower or bachelor's button. Acres and acres of sugar beets, and of flax, and of absinthe. In one valley, some peasants—men and women—were pulling the absinthe and laying it in rows to dry.

"They should burn it instead," Captain Bradstreet remarked rather severely. "The drink they make from absinthe intoxicates and does them much harm."

"But it's a good medicine and brings them a deal of money," said Mr. Rowe.

Farther on, at a turning of the road, Donald gave an ecstatic little scream and pointed with his finger.

"Oh, look, mamma, look!"

An old dame was approaching, leading five cows abreast, all tied together by the horns.

"She seems to be moving her dairy," remarked Kirke to the carriage at large.

"*Her* dairy? The dairy of the whole neighborhood, more likely," said Paul.

"A *cow*-operative dairy," suggested Pauline quickly, whereupon they all laughed.

A little way behind the "co-operative dairy" followed a young peasant woman in a short dress trundling a black baby carriage.

"Think of a solemn black carriage like that for a dear little baby!" exclaimed Mrs. Rowe. "Yet the French are called a cheerful people!"

They passed black Norman carts with enormous wheels, and the carts were drawn by Norman horses with large hairy feet.

"Not a bit like America anywhere," said Kirke, "and I'm glad of it. We came here to see something new."

It was late in the afternoon when The Happy Six and their elders reached the fishing village where they were to spend the night. Its gray stone inn was more than two hundred years old, and like many inns in Europe had once been a castle. There were no carpets, but the floors were spotlessly white, and the copper saucepans and kettles in the kitchen shone through the windows of the room as the setting sun shone through the ruins on the neighboring cliff.

After dinner the gentlemen and lads of the company prowled about these ruins in the twilight, while Pauline and Molly chatted in the inn parlor with three young English girls boarding with their mother in the house.

Miss Evans, wearing the alligator-skin bag, as was her habit, came in to read by the lamp upon the centre-table; but, after Weezy and Donald were in bed, went to assist Mrs.

Rowe in the care of Jane Leonard, who was now suffering severely from headache.

The next day Jane could not raise her head from the pillow. Mrs. Rowe and Miss Evans sat with her by turns, while Donald was left to the care of the rest of the party.

This disposal of himself suited his little lordship, for, everybody's business being nobody's, he was allowed to run at large, and within certain limits do about as he pleased. Captain Bradstreet, Paul, and Kirke had set out early for another peep at the ruins, and as soon as the dew was off the grass Donald slipped away from his father, lounging in front of the hotel, and trudged behind Weezy and the older girls toward the sea.

The beaten path which they followed ended abruptly at the smooth, flat cobble-stones of the shelving beach. Here stood a row of disabled old fishing-boats, drawn up above the dashing of the tide and fashioned into rude cottages, each with a thatched roof, narrow door, and two or three small windows.

It was in these tiny buildings that the fishermen stored their wares. As the children drew near, fish-wives were sitting upon the door-steps of some of the boat-houses, netting seines of coarse green twine. A few of the women wore starched white caps with wide, flopping borders. The rest were bareheaded, and the sun stared saucily down at their shiny red faces.

"Let's speak to the best-looking one, Pauline," suggested Molly, as they sauntered along the row of women.

"To the least ugly one, you mean, don't you?" returned Pauline, casting a scrutinizing glance at the busy workers.

"The least ugly one is that woman straight ahead in the sky-blue apron."

"She has hair on her chin, Polly."

"And haven't they all, or nearly all, you

fastidious creature? And isn't she the only one that looks reconciled to it?" Pauline rattled on. "I think she deserves to be noticed." And stepping up to the peasant, she made a graceful bow, and said,—

"*Bon jour, madame.*"

"*Bon jour, ma'm'selle,*" replied the fish-wife politely, not pausing from her netting. Then nodding toward Donald, she added something about "*le joli petit enfant.*"

"She seems to be delivering an oration, Molly," murmured mischievous Pauline with a serious countenance.

"Don't, Polly, don't make me laugh in her face," entreated Molly, her lips twitching. "She said Donald was a pretty little child. I understood as much as that."

"Pretty? Of course he is, and he's sweet; but that's no reason why she should run her words all together like melted caramels," retorted Pauline, looking straight at the woman and speaking in an easy, conversational tone.

The woman sat there, serenely unconscious that she was talked about, and Molly had to turn away to hide her merriment. It was one of her minor trials that Pauline could, at almost any time, surprise her into a giggle, while remaining herself as sedate as an owl.

As Molly was looking toward the hotel, she happened to espy the three English girls tripping down the path in Indian file, swinging long towels in their hands.

"They are actually going in bathing," said Molly, pretending that this was what she was laughing at.

"*I* want to go bavin'," echoed Donald, hopping up and down on the great loose cobble-stones. "*I* want to go bavin'."

In his excitement he lost his unsteady footing, and pitching headlong into the fish-net, became entangled in it like a fly in a cobweb.

Molly extricated him as deftly and quickly as she could, though this was a work of time, because he struggled and twisted himself about and kept catching his active little fingers in the meshes.

But the annoying little incident had not diverted the boy in the least from his original desire. He was no sooner free than he repeated emphatically, —

"I say, I want to go bavin'."

"Not to-day, precious," answered Molly, smoothing his hair, which the net had tossed this way and that, till the child's head resembled a thistle gone to seed. "We can't any of us go into the ocean to-day, not even Kirke. We didn't bring our bathing-suits with us, you see, Donny."

Her reply provoked from her little brother a heartrending shriek which drew the three English lassies in haste to his side.

"Poor little fellow, we saw him fall into

that net. Is he dreadfully hurt?" cried the eldest, whom her sisters called Edith.

"It is a dreadful thing to fall into the *Seine*," replied Pauline, who never could resist the chance to make a pun.

"No, he was not hurt," said Molly. "Only in his little feelings, because I can't let him go in bathing, Miss Edith. We haven't his bathing-suit here, and if we had, I don't believe mamma would dare let him go into the sea."

"Wouldn't she allow him to take off his shoes and stockings and wade in the shallow water?" asked kind Miss Edith, wishing to see the grieving child happy.

"Mamma would, mamma would," piped Donald, taking it upon himself to answer the question.

"Do you think so, little sailor?"

Miss Edith caressingly touched the embroidered anchor upon the collar of his navy-blue jacket, and turning to Molly said,—

"Because I know of a nice, shallow pool where little ones often wade. It is over there between those two rocks near the foot of the chalk cliffs."

"Thank you, Miss Edith, you're very kind to tell us about it," replied Molly, wiping Donald's eyes, again beginning to twinkle. "You are sure it is perfectly safe?"

"Oh, yes, it's so far from the sea that the waves never wash into it except at high tide."

This was all true; and thinking she had done a kindness to the young Americans, Miss Edith gave them a pleasant nod and followed her sisters to the bath-house lower down the beach, to prepare for a plunge into the ocean.

CHAPTER X

WHERE IS NUMBER SIX?

"COME, go wadin'; Molly, please come," coaxed Donald, pulling at his sister's skirt before the English girls were out of hearing.

"Yes, in a minute, little brother."

Molly lingered to tell the fish-wife in painstaking French that they were sorry to have interrupted her netting.

The woman puzzled over Molly's words as Molly and Pauline had previously puzzled over her own, for the language of Paris is far different from the *patois* of Normandy.

"She looks as black as the boat-house," observed roguish Pauline, at the same time glancing tenderly at the old peasant, as if paying her a compliment.

"You sha'n't guy the poor woman, Polly; that's shabby," expostulated her comrade. "But tell me how to make her understand what I said."

"Smile at her, Molly, and shake your head at Donald, then at the seine. See how that will work."

Apparently it worked well. The fish-wife smiled at Molly in return and spread out the seine to show that it was uninjured.

"It's a minute now!" cried Donald at the end of his scanty allowance of patience. "Please go, Molly, please, please!"

"We're going this very second, Donny; but what a little tease you are!" returned his sister, taking his chubby hand in hers.

Then, bidding adieu to the matron of the quaint, thatched cottage, they all walked down to the beach in the direction pointed out by Miss Edith.

The cobble-stones were rounded and smooth

like paper-weights, and moved beneath their feet with every step. Molly was obliged to support her little brother very carefully to prevent his stumbling, and he dragged so heavily upon her arm that she reached the pool quite fatigued.

Once there, divested of shoes and stockings, and with his sailor trousers rolled above the knee, Donald skipped about in the shoal water, laughing and screaming at the top of his little lungs.

"It's 'most as good as bavin'," he called to Weezy. "Come wade wiv me!"

"Pretty soon," replied Weezy, seating herself upon the rough ledge that separated the pool from the ocean, and beginning to unbutton her boots.

At the second button her hand was arrested by a shout from the summit of the cliff that rose abruptly at her side. It was Kirke's voice, as clear and shrill as a trumpet.

"Come up here, all of you! Come up and see the ruins!"

Pauline sprang in haste from her perch on a rock, crying,—

"We'll do it, Molly, won't we? I'm on tiptoe for it."

All the morning she had been longing to explore this ancient Roman fortress, of which the boys had talked the night before. Her imagination had been revelling in its half-buried donjon, its secret passages and its mouldering lookout, from which, according to Kirke's extravagant statement, they could "almost see the north pole."

And now was the very time to visit the old gray walls; yes, the very time, for her father and Paul and Kirke were wandering up there photographing the ruins, and could help Molly and herself over the risky places. It was a damper to her enthusiasm when Molly sorrowfully replied,—

"You and Weezy can go, Polly, but I can't; I can't leave Donald."

"There'd be no fun without you, Molly." Pauline made a wry face. "Can't we take Donald up with us?"

"Not peaceably, I'm afraid," whispered Molly with a sage smile. "Certainly not just yet."

"Supposing he *should* cry a little; that wouldn't hurt him," persisted Pauline, hard-hearted in her eagerness.

Molly flushed an indignant crimson. "I'm not going to drag my little brother out of the water for anybody," she retorted quickly. "I think 'twould be a burning shame, when he loves it so and has hardly been in it two seconds."

Donald entertained the same opinion, and when Pauline essayed by sweet words to coax him upon dry land, he retreated with all speed to the middle of the pool. This, though scarcely nine feet across and but four inches in depth, was an ocean to him; and from its secure centre he shook his wilful little head at his would-be captor.

His sisters smiled indulgently; but Pauline betrayed an impatience that wounded Molly.

"I want to see the ruins as much as Polly does," she reflected; "but I won't cheat Donald of his little rights."

Then a bright idea occurred to her. "I've a great mind, Pauline, to ask Kirke to come down here and stay with Donny while we go up there."

And she bent her neck backward to gaze to the top of the dizzy height. Upon the side where they stood and also upon the side fronting the ocean the cliff was almost perpendicular.

"Oh, do ask him!" returned Pauline. "He and Paul have been through the fortress twice, and we haven't seen so much as the shed."

"*I'd* scream to him and ask him, Molly," said Weezy, ever free with advice.

"Come up — to see — the ru-ins!" repeated Kirke on a higher key, wondering why they vouchsafed no reply.

"Answer him, Molly, do, or he'll crack the ears of France," cried Pauline at her elbow.

Molly laughed.

"Take pity on me, Miss Ready-wit, and stop being so funny," she entreated, proceeding to make a speaking-tube of her hands, and calling energetically to Kirke, "Will you — come down — to look out — for Donald?"

Though sweet and full, her tones were not very strong. "*Look out*" was all that Kirke could distinguish of her sentence. "Can't hear," he vociferated; "speak louder."

"We'll go — if you'll — *look out* — for *Don!*" shouted Molly explosively, nearly splitting her throat. "*Will you* do it?"

"Of course I will! Come right along!"

thundered Kirke, who had caught a word here and a word there and had "jumped" at his sister's meaning. She wanted him to go with her to the Lookout, that tumble-down tower overlooking the sea. He was sure that was what she wished, for she was always turning giddy in high places and clinging to him, afraid to take a step by herself.

So, not to vex her with needless questions, Kirke simply waved his hand to put an end to the talk, and went back to the lofty tower to mount anew the broken steps within; for he wanted to decide how far up it would be safe for Molly and Pauline and Weezy to climb.

Meanwhile the girls below expected at any moment to see him descending the winding path that led from the chalk cliffs to the fishing village. When he failed to appear, Pauline bethought herself of the secret passages she had heard of. Probably he had chosen one of these to shorten the distance. Why, of course he had, and there was no knowing just where he would come out.

"He must be here soon, Molly," said Pauline impatiently, "and it's getting hotter and hotter. Why can't we be going on slowly?"

"Will you keep Donald happy till Kirke gets here, darling?" asked Molly, smiling at her sister. "If you will, I'll give you a nickel."

"I'll give you another, and that'll be a dime," added Pauline.

Weezy gladly consented to the bargain. She was filling a scrap-book with paper flags of all nations, and a dime would purchase several of these.

"You can run to overtake us, you know, Weezy, as soon as Kirke comes," called Molly from the entrance of the path. "Tell him not to let Donald wade too long."

"I won't forget," screamed Weezy, as the

two girls passed from her view behind a bend in the hill.

At their last glimpse of Donald, he was standing outside the pool with Weezy, looking at some peasant women who were washing at the margin of the beach. The women were kneeling with their backs to the children, rubbing the clothes white upon the smooth stones.

Twenty minutes may have elapsed, and Pauline and Molly were approaching the dry moat, that half surrounded the hoary fortress, when they were startled by piercing shrieks from Weezy, following one another in quick succession.

Shrieking in their turn to Captain Bradstreet and Paul above them, they rushed madly down the descent, and as they drew near the foot, met Weezy herself, sobbing wildly, —

"Donald's drownded. I know he's drownded."

And choking with grief and terror, she faltered out her pitiful story:—

Tired of waiting for Kirke, she had left Donald for "just a teeny second," and skipped away to look at the kneeling washer-women. On her return the child had vanished, and his little blue sailor-suit lay in a tumbled heap upon the brink of the pool.

"Donny had been teasing again to go in bathing, and I wouldn't let him go," wailed his despairing little sister; "so I s'pect when I wasn't there he skipped into the ocean all alone by himself. Donald, Don-*ald*, *where* are you? Oh, dear, dear. I wish I was dead!"

"Run to the inn, Weezy, for papa and mamma; run as fast as you can," cried Molly, in a husky voice.

The sympathetic peasant women, having discovered the cause of the outcry, had deserted their washings and clattered in their hob-nailed shoes toward the base of the cliff, near the tell-tale garments. Here the water was deeper than on the beach in front of the boat-house, and it dashed over a ledge worn into many chambers. The peasants were pointing to these deep chambers with gloomy looks, and muttering low to one another, when Mr. and Mrs. Rowe and Weezy came flying from the inn, and met Captain Bradstreet and the boys upon the shore.

Though pale with anguish, Mrs. Rowe had shed no tears. But when her eyes fell upon the little empty sailor-suit, she gathered it in her arms with the bitter cry, "O Donald, my little Donald, come back to your poor mamma!"

Then it was that something unexpected happened — something which changed her mourning into gladness. A little golden head shot suddenly up from behind a neighboring rock, and a shrill little voice cried out,

"Here I is, mamma. Oh, please come qui-ck."

Everybody jumped as if an earthquake had swallowed the cliff.

"It's Donald, it's Donald! I didn't drown him at all!" shouted Weezy, dancing up and down in frantic joy.

Her mother had rushed behind the sheltering rock to embrace her lost baby.

"Oh, my sweet, cold darling," she cried, pressing the wet child to her breast; "how could you frighten mamma so?"

"Didn't mean to, truly. Was only just a-bavin'," — here disobedient Donald hung his head, — "and Weezy comed back, and then I runned and hid, — just for fun, mamma!"

"But after that, Donald dear, you heard people call to you. Why didn't you answer them and tell them where you were?"

Donald snuggled closer to his mother's breast. "I hadn't a bit o' clo'es on, mamma,

"HERE I IS, MAMMA"

Page 142

don't you know?" he whispered; "not a single bit o' clo'es on! S'pose I wanted the queer old womens to see?"

Mrs. Rowe answered him with a kiss. And when she had hurried on his dry garments, she yielded him up to his father and the rest of the family to be loved and petted, as if he had been a very good instead of a very mischievous little fellow.

CHAPTER XI

WHAT STRANGE COUNTRIES!

"OH, isn't it nice, Molly, that we're all going to *Ruin?*" exclaimed Weezy, giving her sister's hand an ecstatic squeeze under the table.

They were breakfasting again at Hotel Frascati, their party having returned the night before to Havre.

"Don't say *Ruin*, Weezybus! You mix it up with the other ruins; but it's a city, and it's called Rouen," corrected laughing Molly, ending the name with a nasal flourish.

"How silly! I should think they'd know better!" retorted the young American critic. But at the approach of a waiter she immediately became mute. She had a private conviction that these black-coated individuals must comprehend English, they looked so wise.

On leaving the dining-room, Weezy and her friends passed out into the spacious vestibule, and there waited for the carriage which was to convey them to the station. Jane Leonard was with the others, free from headache and keeping a strict watch over frisky little Donald.

As they stood at the foot of the long staircase, the hotel servants — *concierge*, *garçons*, maids in white caps and all — crowded around them.

"They're sorry we're going away, aren't they, Molly? Just as sorry as they can be," whispered gratified Weezy.

"There, you're mistaken, little miss," said Paul, who had overheard the remark. "They're only hanging around for a fee."

"What is a fee, Molly?" questioned Weezy aside.

"Money paid for work, dear. See, papa is

taking out his purse, so is Captain Bradstreet; they're going to give some French coins to the servants."

"To get the servants to move out of the way," interposed Paul archly. "They'll hand each of them a small sum to make them 'move on,' as you do to organ-grinders."

Here the carriage drove up, and the party hastened to catch the train for Rouen. The train was composed of several small black cars or coaches, which Kirke declared looked like a row of Saratoga trunks in mourning. Each coach was divided widthwise into compartments, having on either side a door with a sliding glass panel at the top.

Captain Bradstreet was fortunate enough to secure a vacant compartment which would just accommodate the party, and The Happy Six were soon quietly ensconced in the front seat with their backs toward the engine.

Miss Evans sat opposite Paul and gazed abstractedly out of the window, hardly lifting her eyes from the trim green hedge that bordered the railway track. Once — they were then near Rouen — he saw her start nervously and press her hand to her left side, as if to assure herself that the reticule was in its place.

"How she does clutch that old bag," he whispered in Kirke's ear, as they stopped at the station. "Probably the conductor takes her for a mail-carrier."

"Rouen is a famous old city, Molly; I hope you'll learn all you can about it," said Mr. Rowe wearily, as they alighted at the hotel.

He had not recovered yet from the fatiguing sea voyage, and as soon as they had engaged their rooms at Hotel d'Angleterre, he went to lie down.

When shown to their own apartment,

Molly and Pauline exclaimed at the number of looking-glasses it contained. Even the upper halves of the windows were mirrors; and in trying to gaze out upon the river Seine, Pauline was surprised to see only her own face.

"They want to make the most of their guests, I should say," she remarked dryly, after viewing herself in seven different glasses.

"This might be called 'the chamber of reflection,'" she continued, arranging her crimps.

"You're too bright to live," cried Molly. "But put on your hat again, Miss Vanity. Don't you know we're going to drive around the city?"

"Who are going?"

"Only The Happy Six; that's all."

Their driver was an old man, intelligent and fond of scenery. He took them first through some of the oldest streets of Rouen, hardly six feet wide, where two teams could not possibly pass each other. Perhaps it may have been to warn away other drivers that he cracked his whip so sharply, — "as if he were killing an elephant," Kirke whispered to Paul.

Then they went to see the round tower in which Joan of Arc spent so many tedious months, in a cell only large enough to admit a narrow window, yet with walls twelve feet thick.

Thence they drove to the spot where she was burned as a witch; and Molly stepped from the carriage to read the inscription carved upon the stone in the pavement.

"Oh, how wickedly they did treat that innocent creature!" said she, with flashing eyes. "You know she didn't want to go into battle; but she 'went forth to save France.'"

"And to crown Charles Seventh," added Pauline. "I detest him — the ungrateful thing!"

It was some comfort to the indignant girls to find towers and fountains and streets named for Jeanne D'Arc, and one church sacred to the wonderful maid, where mass is said for soldiers. They came to that in returning from St. Catharine's Hill, from which they had gazed down upon the Seine.

"What a tiny river," said Kirke; "no wider than a New England brook!"

It mattered little to them that Corneille was born at Rouen, and that William the Conqueror died there. Their interest in the history of the city was centred in the trial and martyrdom of Joan the Maid.

Their next resting-place was Mantes, at an old hotel built around an open court — the very court, so Pauline was told, where

William the Conqueror received his death-blow, falling from his horse.

"But I'm thankful to say William didn't die here," said the lively girl, tilting her nose. "They carried him to an abbey at Rouen, where I *hope* 'twas cleaner!"

"But Mantes is an interesting city, anyway," returned Molly dreamily. "Just think, Polly, it's eight hundred years old!"

"Humph! not very forward for its age," sniffed Pauline. "Can't even keep out of the dirt! Mould and antiquity are all very well for those that can afford 'em; as for me, I'm satisfied with simple magnificence."

She found "simple magnificence" a day or two after at the Palace of Versailles, in the Glass Saloon, a ball-room lined with mirrors.

"Yankee Molly, can you believe your ears? The guide-book says this is where Queen Victoria once opened the ball with Napoleon Third!"

And Pauline danced airily across the floor, by way of illustration.

"I hope the queen did it as gracefully as that," replied Molly admiringly. "But oh, Pauline, you haven't seen the splendid 'Court of Marble!' I can show you the balcony above it that poor Marie Antoinette stepped out upon when she tried so hard to pacify that howling mob."

"More than a hundred years ago that was, wasn't it, Molly?" said Pauline, following her. "It makes me feel dreadfully modern, like an hour-old mosquito."

After looking through the famous picture gallery, which so fully illustrates the history of France, the tourists proceeded to Grand Trianon, the palace built by Louis XIV. for Madame de Maintenon. The apartments are all on one floor.

"Perhaps the madame was clumsy and didn't like to climb stairs," suggested Pauline.

Paul and Kirke were delighted with the private rooms of Napoleon First, and with his gorgeous nuptial carriage seen afterwards at the Royal Stables.

But Grand Trianon did not interest any of them as much as did Little Trianon, quarter of a mile away. This is a bewitching toy hamlet in excellent preservation. Here stands the quaint old mill where Louis XVI. played at being miller, and the rustic dairy where his queen, the ill-fated Marie Antoinette, made butter with her own royal hands; and there are modest little houses grouped around the water, like our summer cottages in America.

"Aren't you glad that poor old king and queen had a little fun before they lost their heads?" said Paul.

"If they hadn't lost their heads first, though, they never would have dared risk so much fun," flashed back his sister.

"There seems to have been no end to the

extravagance of the French court in those days. No wonder the people were incensed," remarked Mr. Rowe, as they entered the carriage which was to take them to Paris.

Halfway to the city they paused at the beautiful village of St. Cloud to visit the celebrated park that had once contained a palace, — the favorite resort of royalty.

"Think of the Germans burning it in the late war. What good did that do them?" cried the boys indignantly.

"They're dangerous people, those Germans, always making a smoke," said Pauline, dismissing the topic at the entrance of the Bois de Boulogne.

For miles the road lay through this beautiful forest, no longer as of old haunted by robbers, but now a fashionable park. It was a lovely drive, one never to be forgotten. Even Weezy and Donald were quiet, too fascinated to speak.

It was late in the afternoon when the Silver Gate tourists arrived in "the most beautiful city in the world." On all sides were life and gayety. Everywhere as they passed were little tables along the pavement, and people seated around them eating their suppers and chatting in high, good humor. Weezy wondered aloud if they "ever drank tea in their houses?" Captain Bradstreet said, "Yes, when it rained."

The carriage left our party at an immense hotel, The Continental, which with its six or seven hundred rooms was quite a city in itself.

Here Miss Evans was met by her uncle, and she regretfully took leave of her kind friends. Mrs. Rowe's last words to her were: —

"If you don't succeed with your errand in Paris as you wish, I hope you'll try London. You remember we are to leave here in a fortnight. When our route is decided upon, I'll write you. We should be delighted to have you for a travelling companion again."

As The Happy Six met next morning in the court, Paul announced, —

"The picture galleries and shops and everything will be closed to-day."

"What for, Twinny dear?" asked his sister in an aggrieved tone.

"It's the Fourteenth of July, Better-half, the anniversary of the taking of the Bastille. The French call this their Independence Day, so our *garçon* says. Something like our Fourth of July, I suppose."

"Don't *they* have Fourths of Julys?" put in Weezy. "What funny, funny folks!"

"Their Fourteenth seems to be Memorial Day and Fourth-of-July in one," replied Paul. "Kirke and I are going to *Père la Chaise* this forenoon to see them decorate their soldiers' graves."

As the boys approached this cemetery, the finest in the city, they found the streets on every side filled with dealers in crosses and relics and immortelles; and these sombre tokens which were afterwards placed so tenderly above the sleeping dead were really hideous things.

"Not a single flower or green leaf in them, Molly," said Kirke, on their return, "nothing but wire and tinsel and glass."

But after their mourning duty was performed, the Parisians had a festive time for the rest of the day, dancing on the streets in the evening, — old men and old women, young men and young women, and babies and all.

The whole fortnight in Paris was a giddy whirl of delight to The Happy Six. They drove along the boulevards in *fiacres*, or on the tops of omnibuses. They sailed in pleasure boats on the Seine. They visited churches, palaces, and the tomb of Napoleon. They even ascended to the dizzy summit of the Eiffel Tower which Weezy said "reached 'most to heaven."

Of all the days Donald preferred the last, at the Gardens of Acclimatization. Here he saw animals from every zone, and actually was carried on an ostrich's back.

The children would all have liked a longer time in the beautiful white city, but Mr. Rowe was in haste to reach the baths of Baden Baden.

On the morning of their departure the Silver Gate people were joined at the railroad station by Miss Evans, who shook hands with them all very cordially.

"You perceive I've accepted your kind invitation and am going on to London with you," she said to Mrs. Rowe.

And, tapping her reticule with her gloved finger, she added a few words, inaudible to the rest.

CHAPTER XII

THE VERY HAPPY SIX

"SEE, she's tacked on that everlasting bag again, Molly," whispered Pauline, as the train started. "It always reminds me of a great tag on a little parcel, as if Miss Evans had been done up to be sent by express."

That night they reached Besançon, an old Roman city just under the wall of the Jura Mountains. The hotel at which they stopped was very curious, with sleeping-rooms tucked away here and there, like swallows' nests in a bank. Sometimes these rooms were entered from within the house, sometimes from without, by sly, crooked stairways.

Molly and Pauline could see no beds in their apartment, and ran after the porter to ask him where they were to sleep.

He smiled rather patronizingly, and threw open some unsuspected doors in the partition, which had been concealed by the flowery wall-paper. Inside were two single bedsteads, with maroon curtains of damask, and on each bed was the usual little down quilt called a *duvet*, which had an inconvenient habit of crawling off upon the floor whenever the occupant of the bed turned over.

Altogether the hotel was very quaint, and so completely surrounded by tall buildings that it rarely saw the sun.

"Papa says the house is centuries old," said Molly, throwing up their narrow window.

"Well, we might have known it," replied the ready Pauline. "We might have known it was built in the dark ages by the lack of light in it."

"Papa says Victor Hugo was born in this city," returned Molly. "We're all going by and by to see his old house, and we'll photograph it."

Next day the party drove in carriages through the lovely valley of the Loire to the bewitching little village of Mouthier, where there are no streets to mention, the houses being scattered around in clusters, "as if," as Kirke said, they had been "shaken out of a pepper-box."

Here they visited a cheese-factory, in what had once been a convent, and they declared they should never want any more French cheese; but they forgot this afterward.

To tell of all their travelling experiences would weary you. How they drove through tunnels and around the brink of precipices, to see the Loire rush out from its mountain cave a full-grown river.

How in Switzerland they climbed the Alps on wise-looking little donkeys, took a peep at the yellow stone city of Neuchâtel, once peopled by the Lake-dwellers, and looked down into the bear-pits of Berne.

How in Germany they spent weeks in Baden Baden, and Mr. Rowe was benefited by the mud-baths, which in Weezy's opinion were not at all clean.

How in approaching Cologne they passed vast grain-fields, where the wheat had been reaped and stacked into piles shaped like little woodsheds.

How in Cologne they spent much time in its cathedral, — the finest Gothic cathedral in the world. Paul and Molly never tired of gazing at its graceful arches, its clustered columns and beautiful pictured windows of stained glass.

Kirke and Pauline, however, were more fascinated by the scene in front of their hotel, the Victoria.

It chanced to be market morning, and the peasant women had flocked into the city before sunrise, pushing before them hand-carts filled with fruit and vegetables. Large dogs were harnessed underneath many of these carts, and trotted contentedly with their burdens to the open square, where they either lay down to rest, or stood howling and barking by fifties, while their mistresses chattered and laughed, and spread out their wares to attract customers.

It was while still in Germany that the Americans took a carriage drive along the banks of the Rhine to visit a grim, feudal castle covered with ivy and surrounded by a moat. The castle was the residence of an absent count, and was kept open by servants, who, for a small fee, would show the interior to visitors.

"What a lovely, mouldy old place!" exclaimed Pauline, when the horses had stopped before it. And springing to the ground she hastened into the court, across what formerly had been a drawbridge.

Miss Evans followed more slowly, pausing

midway to peep over the rail down into the sluggish water of the moat beneath her. Owing to a vegetable growth upon its surface, this water was as green and velvety as a meadow.

"I should think that pasture-y look would fool near-sighted cows, shouldn't you, Miss Evans?" said Kirke at her elbow; and he was gratified that she positively laughed at his nonsense. This made the second time she had laughed that day. Entranced by the beauty and antiquity of the spot, she ran about the park with Weezy like a gay young girl; stopped at the ponds to feed from her own luncheon the gold-fish and swans; and on returning to the castle waved her handkerchief from its highest turret.

"She actually looks happy, Polly," observed Molly, answering the salute from the bridge below.

"So she does. She must have forgotten

herself," responded Pauline with a touch of sarcasm.

Pauline was right. Miss Evans *had* forgotten herself, and for this reason something very sad had occurred — something which little Miss Weezy was the first to recognize.

She sat opposite Miss Evans in the carriage, and after they had driven several miles toward Cologne suddenly exclaimed, —

"Why, how funny, Miss Evans! You haven't brought your reticule!"

The young lady flashed a glance at her belt and threw up both hands with a cry.

"What shall I do? What shall I do? I've lost my bag! I had it when we started, and now it is gone!"

"Edward," exclaimed Mrs. Rowe to her husband, "please ask the coachman to turn the carriage about. We must drive back for the reticule at once. I've told you of its valuable contents."

"Family heirlooms probably," reflected Captain Bradstreet. "What was the girl thinking of to carry such trinkets about her person?"

"Do you recollect where you last saw the reticule, Miss Evans?" asked Mr. Rowe, when the horses were retracing their steps.

"Oh, I can't remember, Mr. Rowe!" Miss Evans's face was ghastly white. "I haven't the remotest idea. How could I — how could I have forgotten that reticule for one moment?"

"Don't worry, Miss Evans; we'll find it for you," called Kirke from his seat beside the coachman. "Paul and I will find it for you, if we kill ourselves running."

But though the boys hunted diligently, and the whole party aided in the quest, twilight fell, and the reticule had not been discovered.

They had searched the highway leading to the castle; had searched the castle itself, and questioned the apple-cheeked serving-maid, who had just shown them its interior; had searched the park, and even the ponds within it; and at last had met in despair upon the bridge that spanned the moat.

"I think I must have dropped my reticule into this water when I leaned over the rail here this afternoon," said Miss Evans, her voice quivering. "In that case, the manuscript would be spoiled before now."

"Let's take another look for it in the park; it's lighter there," whispered Kirke to Paul; from no expectation of finding the coveted object where it had been so patiently sought, but from a strong desire to get out of the way before Miss Evans began to cry. Like boys in general, he had a great aversion to seeing a woman in tears.

"Have you a copy of the book, Miss Evans?" asked Mrs. Rowe, as the boys were walking away unobserved.

"Not one line, Mrs. Rowe. My father, by

mistake, destroyed the rough draft when he was burning up old papers."

"I pity you with all my heart, dear friend," said Mrs. Rowe, deeply moved. "But don't be discouraged. It is too dark to look longer now, but we will come back to-morrow."

"O Mrs. Rowe, if I had only listened to you, and sent it by express!" wailed Miss Evans. "But I had too much sentiment. That book was my father's life-work, and I couldn't bear to trust it out of my sight."

"I'm very sorry for you, Miss Evans," observed Captain Bradstreet, adding mentally, "sorry, too, that you should have been so foolish."

"It is too dreadful!" The young lady could no longer restrain her tears. "O Captain Bradstreet, to think that the precious manuscript should have been lost by me, papa's own daughter!"

"I'VE FOUND IT!"

Page 169

"Miss Evans had failed to make satisfactory arrangement for bringing out the book in Paris, Captain Bradstreet," explained Mrs. Rowe. "Consequently, she was taking it to publishers in London."

"It's a sad loss, a sad loss," returned the captain, as he helped the ladies into the carriage. "But where are the rest of us?" he added. "We can't leave our boys."

"They're coming, they're running like everything," cried Weezy, standing upon the wagon-seat to look. "Kirke is holding something up high, and shaking it."

"It's a bag!" shouted Molly, clapping her hands. "I do believe it's Miss Evans's bag!"

"I've found it! Found it just outside the park," yelled Kirke, when within hearing distance. "It's all right. The dew hasn't hurt it!"

It seems that in leaving the park Kirke had seen the glitter of steel under the luxuriant ivy at its entrance, and stooping to brush aside the vines, had touched the clasp of the lost reticule.

"I suppose the chain caught upon the fence when you squeezed through that narrow gap, Miss Evans," said he, in winding up his story.

"Yes, Miss Evans, it must have caught and twitched your bag off so quickly that you didn't know it," added Paul, as the carriage rolled on; "and then the bag fell into that tangle of leaves where nobody noticed it but Kirke. His eyes are as sharp as a razor."

"Fortunately for me, Paul!" Miss Evans was half-laughing, half-crying. "O Kirke, I can't be grateful enough to you for bringing this back to me!"

Kirke blushed with pleasure, and Paul felt a momentary pang of regret that he had not discovered the valued article himself.

He looked on with interest as Miss Evans drew from the alligator-skin bag a parcel neatly encased in oiled silk. It was her father's manuscript, written in a fine clear hand, upon very thin commercial paper.

"Untouched, uninjured! This is more than I deserve!" she exclaimed joyfully.

"Good! Three cheers for the finder! Nine cheers for the owner!" cried Paul, swinging his cap.

And The Happy Six joined in a gay hurrah.

We might follow the glad children over Europe and back again to their sunny home on the Pacific; but perhaps it is better to leave them right here, for then we end the book as we began it, with a chorus of children giving three cheers.

Only Dollie

By Nina Rhoades Illustrated by Bertha Davidson
Square 12mo Cloth $1.00

THIS is a brightly written story of a girl of twelve, who, when the mystery of her birth is solved, like Cinderella, passes from drudgery to better circumstances. There is nothing strained or unnatural at any point. All descriptions or portrayals of character are life-like, and the book has an indescribable appealing quality which wins sympathy and secures success.

"It is delightful reading at all times."—*Cedar Rapids (Ia.) Republican.*

"It is well written, the story runs smoothly, the idea is good, and it is handled with ability.—*Chicago Journal.*

The Little Girl Next Door

By Nina Rhoades Large 12mo Cloth Illustrated by Bertha Davidson $1.00

A DELIGHTFUL story of true and genuine friendship between an impulsive little girl in a fine New York home and a little blind girl in an apartment next door. The little girl's determination to cultivate the acquaintance, begun out of the window during a rainy day, triumphs over the barriers of caste, and the little blind girl proves to be in every way a worthy companion. Later a mystery of birth is cleared up, and the little blind girl proves to be of gentle birth as well as of gentle manners.

Winifred's Neighbors

By Nina Rhoades Illustrated by Bertha G. Davidson Large 12mo Cloth $1.00

LITTLE Winifred's efforts to find some children of whom she reads in a book lead to the acquaintance of a neighbor of the same name, and this acquaintance proves of the greatest importance to Winifred's own family. Through it all she is just such a little girl as other girls ought to know, and the story will hold the interest of all ages.

For sale by all booksellers, or sent postpaid on receipt of price by the publishers

LOTHROP, LEE & SHEPARD CO., BOSTON

www.ingramcontent.com/pod-product-compliance
Lightning Source LLC
Chambersburg PA
CBHW022358020726
47500CB00002B/344

* 9 7 8 3 3 3 7 4 0 7 6 2 9 *